I0640826

Alfred Woltmann, Joseph Cundall

Hans Holbein

Alfred Woltmann, Joseph Cundall

Hans Holbein

ISBN/EAN: 9783337394868

Printed in Europe, USA, Canada, Australia, Japan

Cover: Foto ©Andreas Hilbeck / pixelio.de

More available books at **www.hansebooks.com**

"The whole world without Art would be one great wilderness."

HANS HOLBEIN

FROM "HOLBEIN UND SEINE ZEIT," BY DR. ALFRED WOLTMANN.

BY JOSEPH CUNDALL

Author of "The Life and Genius of Rembrandt."

LONDON

SAMPSON LOW, MARSTON, SEARLE, & RIVINGTON, LTD.

St. Dunstan's House

FETTER LANE, FLEET STREET, E.C.

1892

6

THE PEASANTS' DANCE.

PREFACE.

ENGLISH artists have never fully acknowledged the debt they owe to the memory of Hans Holbein. It was he who first raised the art of painting to perfection in this country, and it may be questioned if, in many of the finest requirements of portraiture, his work has ever been excelled.

The bold touches of the well-known Windsor portraits show unmistakeably the vigour of a master's hand. They are drawn by one who had no doubt of his power, and are marvellous examples of swift dexterity.

As a colourist Holbein claims admission into the first rank of painters. Those who have seen his finest portraits—most of which were painted in England, but are now scattered among the galleries of Europe—acknowledge his wonderful gift of placing before our eyes the very man he wishes to present. Mr. Ruskin praises some of his portraits with the greatest enthusiasm, and every art-critic who has carefully examined Holbein's pictures has been charmed with the excellence of his workmanship

His altar-piece at Darmstadt—better known to the world by the excellent copy at Dresden—was painted before he was thirty years of age, yet it ranks next to the work of Raphael: and there can be little doubt that had the grand picture of "The Family of Sir Thomas More" been preserved to this time, we should have possessed a group of portraits, which, both in composition and painting, would have been of surpassing interest and of the greatest merit.

As an ornamentist none has excelled him. His drawing, in the Bodleian Library, of Queen Jane Seymour's cup is pre-eminent in its art; and the designs for jewellery and decorations of every kind in the British Museum and at Basel are more to be admired than the works of any of his celebrated countrymen.

The genius of Holbein must undoubtedly have had great influence over English art of the sixteenth century. Previous to his time portrait painting was scarcely known: decoration in various ways was the principal work of the artists of the Court—and in this probably Holbein helped—but no well-authenticated portrait of merit by any known painter before him has yet been found.

From the fountain-head of Hans Holbein there has run one unbroken stream—to which foreign artists have often contributed—which has steadily flowed on until it has increased to the present wide expanse of British art. The painters of England ought certainly to erect a statue to his memory.

With the exception of a few additions which have been

suggested to me by the study of many years, I am indebted for all tho main facts in the present little treatise to the well-known work, "Holbein und seine Zeit," by Dr. Woltmann, who has made an exhaustive study of his subject. His book fills 760 large pages of closely-printed matter, and it has been no easy task to extract the most salient information from such an immense amount of learning. Without the assistance of my friend Mrs. Ruutz Rees, who kindly translated much of the German work for me, I could not have undertaken the labour.

We know little of the life of Holbein apart from his works, but we may rest assured that Dr. Woltmann has left no stone unturned in his endeavours to secure every possible source of knowledge.

J. C.

Surbiton Hill, July, 1879.

THE FOX-CHASE.

CONTENTS.

CHAPTER I.

PAGE

The influence of the Reformation on Art—Augsburg in 1490—The Holbein Family—Ambrosius and Hans Holbein—Their visit to Basel—Employed by Froben the printer—The Zurich table—Erasmus—The "Praise of Folly"—Burgomaster Meyer—1497 to 1516 1

CHAPTER II.

Wall-painting at Lucerne—Portrait of Amerbach—Wall-painting in Basel—The old Town-hall—The Dance of Death—Bible Cuts—Title-pages—Altar-pieces—1517 to 1521 14

CHAPTER III.

The Solothurn and the Meyer Madonna—Portraits of Melancthon and Erasmus—Letter of Erasmus to Sir Thomas More—Disturbances at Basel—Contemplated Journey to England—1522 to 1526 33

CHAPTER IV.

Holbein's first Visit to London—Sir Thomas More's house and family—Portraits of More, Archbishop Warham, and Bishop Fisher—Other portraits—1527 to 1528 46

CHAPTER V.

PAGE

The family of Sir Thomas More—Holbein's visit to Basel—His wife and children—Decorates the Town-hall—Returns to England—Merchants of the Steel-yard—Marriage of Henry VIII. to Anne Boleyn—Portraits of the English nobility—1528 to 1533 54

CHAPTER VI.

Death of Sir Thomas More—Death of Anne Boleyn—Marriage of Henry VIII. to Jane Seymour—The Windsor Drawings—Death of Jane Seymour—The Duchess of Milan—Holbein's Salary—1534 to 1537 80

CHAPTER VII.

Visit to Basel—Death of Sigismund Holbein—Return to England—Portraits of the Prince Edward—Anne of Cleves—Duke of Norfolk—Lady Catherine Howard—Lady Catherine Parr—The Barber-Surgeons' Company—Death of Holbein—His last Will—1538 to 1543 93

Appendix—Notes 105

List of Holbein's Paintings and Drawings . . . 107

Chronology of Hans Holbein 113

Index 115

LIST OF ILLUSTRATIONS.

	Page
Hans Holbein. *From the painting in the Uffizi Gal.* *Frontispiece.*	
Kunz von der Rosen.	4
The Annunciation to the Virgin	5
Saint Barbara—Saint Elizabeth	5
"The Praise of Folly," Illustrations to. (*Two cuts.*)	9
Pilate washing his hands	12
The Peasants' Dance	14
Two Soldiers. (*Design for glass-painting.*)	18
Dance of Death. (*Eight cuts.*)	20
Study of Costume	24
Old Testament Pictures. (*Four cuts.*)	28
The Meyer Madonna. (*Two pages.*)	35
Hans Holbein. *From the drawing at Basel*	40
German Ship of the 16th Century	45
The Fox-chase	46
Archbishop Warham	51
The Family of Sir Thomas More	56
Henry VIII.	64
Portrait of an Englishman	70
Henry VIII. and his Father	80
Hubert Morett, the Goldsmith	86
Anne of Cleves	96
Duke of Norfolk	100

BIBLIOGRAPHY.

List of the most important modern works on Holbein.

HOLBEIN UND SEINE ZEIT. Des Künstler's Familie, Leben und Schaffen. Von Alfred Woltmann. Second Edition in two volumes. With illustrations. Leipzig, 1874-6.

—— English Translation of the First Edition, by F. E. Bunnett. With sixty illustrations. London, 1872.

SOME ACCOUNT OF THE LIFE AND WORKS OF HANS HOLBEIN, PAINTER OF AUGSBURG. By Ralph Nicholson Wornum, Keeper and Secretary, National Gallery. London, 1867.

HANS HOLBEIN DER JÜNGERE. Von J. S. Wesseley. In "Kunst und Künstler," von Dr. Robert Dohme. Leipzig, 1876.

JEAN HOLBEIN (dit le Jeune). Par Charles Blanc. In "Histoire des Peintres de toutes les Écoles." Paris, 1860.

HANS HOLBEIN. Par Paul Mantz. Dessins et Gravures sous la direction de Edouard Lièvre. Folio. Paris, 1879.

ERGÄNZUNGEN UND NACHWEISUNGEN ZUM HOLZSCHNITTWERK HANS HOLBEINS DES JÜNGEREN. Von Prof. Salomon Vögelin in Zurich. In "Repertorium für Kunstwissenschaft." Stuttgart, 1879.

DIE GRAPHISCHEN KÜNSTE. Redigirt von Dr. Oskar Berggruen. Wien 1879. (In which will be found an etching of "The Zurich Table.")

HANS HOLBEIN.

CHAPTER I.

The influence of the Reformation on Art—Augsburg in 1490.—The Holbein Family—Ambrosius and Hans Holbein—Their visit to Basel—Employed by Froben the printer—The Zurich table—Erasmus—The "Praise of Folly"—Burgomaster Meyer.

1497 TO 1516.

THE close of the fifteenth century marked the transition from the darkness of the Middle Ages to the more enlightened days of the Reformation.

The growing influences of the time, seconded by the invention of printing, can be traced in the writings, the handicrafts, and especially in the arts of the century. Architecture, chief exponent of the beliefs of the people, changed its character; sculpture became more refined, and as in the palmy days of Athens, more decorative; and painting made rapid strides. The emancipation from ecclesiastical thraldom, which was the necessary result of the continued agitation of the period, exercised an enormous influence upon the artists of every school, who, by a natural transition, returned to the study of the early and almost forgotten Masters.

Hence began the culture of Art which we call Renaissance. The goldsmiths assumed a rank they had never before held: and the art of engraving, which attained at the same time a pre-eminence and importance altogether new, became a powerful instrument in the diffusion of knowledge. The onward movement, commencing in Italy, spread with an increasing force over the continent of Europe; and in Germany, but more especially in Suabia, its influence was very widely felt.

One of the foremost pioneers of the new school was the celebrated Martin Schongauer, a painter so esteemed by his compatriots as to be constantly called the "Glory of Painters." Belonging to the old Flemish school, his pictures exhibit all the newly-awakened realistic ideas of the Netherlands, and are at the same time marked by the ideality of German art. His influence upon his successors cannot be exaggerated, and to him and an equally celebrated painter of the same epoch, Hans Burgkmair of Augsburg,[1] may undoubtedly be ascribed much of the wonderful perfection of the renowned Hans Holbein the younger, whose fame excelled that of any of his countrymen.

Of all the Suabian cities, Augsburg at this time took the lead, and under the enlightened rule of the Emperor Maximilian made the most rapid strides in intellectual advancement. Situated upon one of the highest spurs of the Bavarian mountains, her position in a military point of view was important; and being on the high road to the

[1] Schongauer died in 1488; Burgkmair in 1531.

Alps and Italy, she enjoyed close and constant communication with the cultured Italians. Here, quite at the close of the fifteenth century, probably in 1497, Hans Holbein the younger was born.[1]

We can trace his genealogy back for two generations. From the tax registers of Augsburg we learn that one Michael Holbein, a leather-seller, first settled in that city in 1451. He must have been a man of some little substance, as we find he possessed plots of land in various parts of the town, and that his name and also his wife's occur in several of the public records of the period. He had two sons—Hans, who may have been born about 1460, and Sigismund, who was probably a few years younger. Both became paintors. Sigismund left his native town and settled in Berne.[2] Hans, we know from the city registers, resided at Augsburg at intervals for many years. It was at one time said that he married a daughter of Burgkmair, but this has been ascertained to be an error. We learn that he was made a citizen of Ulm in 1499, and two years later that he visited Frankfort.

Many of the paintings of Hans Holbein the elder can be traced. He excelled in portraiture, and, after the fashion of his time, often introduced likenesses into his pictures. In one of these, the 'Life of St. Paul,' he has given figures of himself and his two sons, Ambrosius and Hans. Upon the head of the younger his hand rests lightly, as though in recognition of the budding talent of the boy. We can recognize in the child's round bright face, pretty open eyes and expression, the traits which we find in a later sketch by the father of the younger Hans

---

[1] Appendix, Note I. [2] Sigismund Holbein died in 1540.

and his brother. Of the boyhood and youth of Hans and his brother Ambrosius nothing absolutely certain is known, but much may be inferred.

KUNZ VON DER ROSEN.

From a drawing by Holbein the elder, in the Berlin Gallery.

A few sketches in silver point, now in the Berlin Museum, were at one time attributed to Hans the younger, but later authority has decided that they were the production of the elder Hans. They give evidence of the existence in the father of the same kind of genius as that which renders his son's name immortal.

Many other sketches and paintings have been attributed to the son which the recently discovered date of his birth renders it impossible for us to claim for him.

THE ANNUNCIATION.

From the Saint Sebastian altar-piece by Hans Holbein the elder, at Munich.

Foremost amongst these is the altar-piece of St. Sebastian in Munich, which is now acknowledged to be the crowning work of the elder Holbein. The wings of this altar-piece are especially well designed. On one is a picture of the 'Annunciation;' on the other are graceful figures of 'St. Barbara' and 'St. Elizabeth.' These are decorated with renaissance ornament, which his son Hans afterwards so frequently introduced.

That the youths Ambrosius and his brother Hans early knew the meaning of hard work and had practical experience of privation is probable, as from certain evidence we find that their father was constantly summoned for the payment of insignificant sums. Thus it stands upon record that on the 10th of May, 1515, he was sued by a creditor for the moderate sum of one florin, and again in the following year a demand was entered against him for only thirty-two kreutzers. After the year 1516 he is named in the tax register as living at a short distance from Augsburg; and one year later his own brother, Sigismund, appears against him in court with a claim for some thirty-four florins, which he states were advanced to enable Hans Holbein to convey his painting materials to Eygznen, that is, to Isenheim in Alsace.

Once more, in the year 1521, the unfortunate painter is sued for forty-one kreutzers. In 1524 his name appears for the last time in the Augsburg tax register, and in the same year he is entered in the *Handwerke buch der Maler* as among the dead.

From these varied sources it is clear that Ambrosius and Hans could have received little material assistance from their father. It is more than probable that he made free use of their labour in his studio, and it may well be conceived that some of the paintings now attributed to him were indebted in some measure to the talents of his gifted son. All that we positively know is that both brothers were in Basel in the year 1515. At that period we find records of paintings executed by Hans, and in the following year an account of the productions of Ambrosius. Probably they paid their first visit to Basel during the year which they spent in travel in accordance with the fashion of the time.

The quiet burgher town of Basel was at this time a market for all talent. The home of many of the most illustrious writers and thinkers of the day, Basel offered an asylum to those whose advanced opinions made them unwelcome in Germany or elsewhere. Its University, already famous, drew to its walls all who sought after knowledge, and a chronicler of the day, exulting in the advancement of the inhabitants, remarks that in the whole town there was not to be found a house which did not contain a learned or a celebrated man. The advancement in the arts of copper-plate engraving, etching, and wood-engraving opened new sources of gain to the artist. A constant demand for illustrations, and for title-pages, or for initial letters of books, offered more plentiful and productive occupation than any to be found in Suabia. We find Hans Holbein speedily employed, although his earliest known production was only a schoolmaster's signboard; rough and rude in workmanship, it yet gave evidence of the master mind.

Two portraits in the Basel Gallery are also attributed to him at this time: the one, a woman's head with childish lineaments; the other, a man's, with clear, sharp features and lively expression. It is probable, however, that his first stay in Basel, although it had a vital influence upon his

SAINT BARBARA. SAINT ELIZABETH.

From the Saint Sebastian altar-piece by Hans Holbein the elder, at Munich.

fortunes, was of short duration, for while we find but slight mention of him between the years 1515 and 1520, his brother Ambrosius is already mentioned as a citizen in 1517, which conveys the idea that he was alone, and that his brother was travelling.

This is confirmed by the number of paintings in other towns which can be traced to Hans Holbein, more especially by one on a large table in Zurich which still bears the signature of "Hans Ho."[1] There is no doubt that this was executed in 1515, because at the right-hand corner of the table can still be seen the coats of arms of the Ber and Brunner families. It was painted for Hans Ber, who married a certain Barbara Brunner on the 24th of June, 1515, and who fell in the battle of Marignano on the 14th of September in the same year. Sandrart, who gives a good description of this table, considers it to be entirely the work of Hans Holbein the younger. In it "St. Nobody" is depicted with a most desolate countenance. In the midst of ruins, broken porcelain, glass, and torn books, he sits on a tub, his mouth padlocked. The whole representation is extremely graphic. An open letter, on which HANS HOLBEIN is written, lies so naturally on the table, that many people have attempted to take it up. Writing materials and spectacles are painted in the same natural manner. The production is divided into two parts, one forming the centre portion of the table, and the other the border, upon which can still be deciphered the remnants of an old German verse, celebrating the "Nobody" who is always responsible for household breakages. Striking as the painting is as a whole, it is no less happy in its details; for example, a lady with a falcon on a wonder-

---

[1] Appendix, Note II.

fully foreshortened horse. The whole work is full of merry conceits and allusions to the wit of the day.

A much better example of the same style of art is to be found in the pen-and-ink illustrations of Erasmus's "Praise of Folly," which brought Hans into communication with the greatest thinker of the century. Erasmus, renowned throughout Europe for his learning, first visited Basel in 1513. His acquaintance with Froben, who published his "Adagia" and his translation of the New Testament, led him there in the first instance. His arrival was anxiously looked for by Froben, and a charming anecdote is related of their first meeting. Erasmus introduced himself to the famous printer as his own messenger, but in his excitement in discussing his published works, he failed to carry out his assumed character. Froben recognized him, joyfully welcomed him, and refused to allow him to return to his inn. In his subsequent visits to Basel, Erasmus uniformly made use of Froben's house, until he rented one for himself in 1521. But from his first arrival in Basel his interest in that city and its inhabitants continued unabated.

Whether we consider the fact that Holbein illustrated his "Praise of Folly" as an evidence that they were acquainted, or whether we suppose that Erasmus gave the order for the sketches in the first instance through Froben or some other friend, it is equally certain that the young painter brought a keen appreciation of the wit of the writer to the execution of his task.

Moreover, his illustrations show an acquaintance with both Latin and Greek, which argues well for his mental attainments. For instance, when the expression *mutuum muli scabunt* occurs, Holbein interprets it upon the margin by two asses rubbing against each other. And where mythological expressions are used, he invariably explains them rightly. Allusion being made to Vulcan and to Penelope's web, the characters appear delineated by him in suitable attitude and costume. When the clamour of the priests, ceasing only when a morsel is thrown to them, is satirically spoken of, and the commentator relates how Æneas quieted Cerberus by a sop, the painter, following out the idea, depicts Æneas in knight's costume with a switch in his hand, holding out a sausage to a three-

THE END OF FOLLY'S SERMON.

headed hell-hound. Throughout the volume such evidence of Holbein's ability to construe classical allusions is constantly shown.

The illustrations of this famous satire were as deservedly popular as the work itself. Erasmus wrote nothing else in the same strain, but he was never more successful. The book went through twenty-seven editions during its author's lifetime, and Holbein undoubtedly deserves an equal share of its popularity. Throughout its pages his genial hearty humour asserted itself—in one case, unfortunately, to the detriment of his reputation. The name of Erasmus having occurred in the text, the artist introduced a sketch of him on the margin, making him appear much younger than he was at the time. The author jestingly retaliated by turning the page and writing the name "Holbein" beside a passage from Horace: "A fat pig from the flock of Epicurus." The illustration represented a wild fellow sitting at a well-spread board drinking! This joke has been interpreted to mean that Hans was given to drink. That he was full of humour and intense appreciation of life, his works sufficiently testify; but it is equally certain that had his conduct been in any way disgraceful he could never have retained the friendship and esteem of such men as Erasmus, Amerbach and Froben.

FOLLY GAMBLING.

To the early period of his first visit to Basel, 1516, belong the portraits of the burgomaster Jacob Meyer, called Meyer of Hasen, and his second wife. If we are delighted with the life and humour of his pen-and-ink sketches, we find still deeper evidence of his genius in these pictures. We detect in them the advancement we traced in the later works of the father, and they especially recall the two heads in the St. Sebastian altar-piece.

Burgomaster Meyer was a great man in the city. The qualities that distinguished him are sufficiently proved by the position he held during such troubled times. The first of the commonalty elected to this responsible office, he was often re-elected and, during his term of office some five years later, both bishops and knights were shorn of many of their privileges. His countenance, as preserved to us by Holbein's pencil, portrays the energy and determination which characterized him. The expression of the mouth, with its lightly closed lips, is extremely full of life and meaning. The gold coin in his hand has historical significance, for it is one of the new issue by the Emperor Maximilian, and bears the stamp of 1516. The monogram and date introduced into the architecture in the background give the same year. The frame enclosing this portrait contains the companion likeness of his young wife. Burgomaster Meyer married, in the first instance, a sister of the very Hans Ber for whom Hans Holbein painted the table in Zürich, and who no doubt introduced the artist to the burgomaster. The second wife, Dorothea Kannegiesser, is painted as still very young. Her pleasing features are noteworthy for the modesty of expression which gives them so much charm. The exquisite skill of the artist is shown in the elaboration of every detail in the rich embroidery of her attire. Deep black and red play a prominent part in the painting, yet are in perfect harmony with the warm but somewhat brown flesh-tints and the light blue atmosphere, which, with the architectural framework, forms the background. The earlier sketches in silver pencil of both these portraits may be seen in the Basel collection. In that of the burgomaster, his curly hair is wonderfully drawn. Both sketches have notes on the margin as to colour of the hair and eyes,[1] by which means Holbein spared his sitters many tedious hours.

To this year, 1516, belongs the portrait of Hans Herbster, a painter of whose productions little is known. Striking in appearance, he is represented in a dark painter's coat and red cap, with long hair and full beard. A frame with its renaissance carving and columns, with sportive genii clambering up them, surrounds the portrait, and gives, beside the name, the information that he was OPORINI PATER,—father of the celebrated printer Oporinus. This picture is now in the possession of the Earl of Northbrook.

Under the date 1517 we find another work attributed to Holbein. It is evidently a very early one, and represents half-length pictures of Adam and Eve—Adam with a flowing beard, and Eve with features greatly resembling the head of a saint. To the same year we must also assign five representations of the 'Passion,' very coarsely painted upon linen. The two best of them are attributed to Hans, and there is some reason to suppose that the others were the work of Ambrosius. They bear a close resemblance to his known productions, more particularly on account of the dark colour of the background. It is possible that they were the joint work of the brothers, hastily executed for some religious ceremony. Copies of seven of these drawings are in the British Museum, executed with a pen and washed with Indian ink.

Little is authentically known of the works of Ambrosius, with the exception of his later drawings for illustrations. A small tablet in the Basel Museum is assigned to him. It is the representation of the Saviour as the Man of Sorrows

[1] Similar notes occur on the Windsor drawings.

PILATE WASHING HIS HANDS.

From the drawings of "The Passion," in the Basel Museum.

after Dürer's Passion-scene, but it is not successful. The treatment of the subject is weak, the colouring neither so warm nor so natural as in his brother's works, but his child-angels are admirable. Two portraits of little boys in yellow frocks are also ascribed to him. The painting is thin, light, and tender, free from the harsh outlines of some of his earlier works. There exist also a very primitive representation of a fair young lady in a grey dress, with the initials H.V. on her locket, and a portrait of Jörg Schweiger, the goldsmith, which many ascribe to Ambrosius. In the Darmstadt Gallery we find a picture of a fair young man in a scarlet cloak and hat, with a blue background, which is marked "H. 1515 H." Probably, the first H should have been an A, as the painting bears no resemblance to anything either of Hans Holbein or of his father. Ambrosius must also claim the merit of a picture in the Hermitage at St. Petersburg, although it is catalogued as being a work by Hans Holbein, "not equal in execution to his others." We have few traces of any later paintings by Ambrosius, but in several books published by Froben and Andreas Cratander at this time we find his initials on elaborate designs engraved on wood for the title-pages of books by Erasmus and others. The latest of these is dated 1519. Ambrosius figures in the Basel law-courts as a witness in 1516, and in 1517 he was made free of the Painters' Guild; but as we hear no more of him nor of his works after the year 1519 we may conjecture that he probably died young.

THE PEASANTS' DANCE.

CHAPTER II.

Wall-painting at Lucerne—Portrait of Amerbach—Wall-painting in Basel—The old Town hall—The Dance of Death—Bible Cuts—Title-pages—Altar-pieces.

1517 TO 1521.

WE have evidence that in 1517 Hans Holbein was living in Lucerne. In the register of the Guild of St. Luke it is stated that he made a donation of one florin to that society; and in the town records he appears as fined for taking part in a quarrel on the 10th of December of that year.

About this time Hans was employed by the mayor of Lucerne, Herr Herstenstein, to decorate his house with wall-paintings within and without. In this undertaking Hans found full scope for his genius, and although, unfortunately, the house was destroyed at the beginning of the present century to make way for modern structures, we can obtain some idea of the execution of his task from copies which still exist. Wall-painting was not greatly esteemed in Germany and Switzerland at this time; there was none of the elaboration we meet with in Italian interiors of that period, or in those of a later date. The work was little valued and very badly paid; but we find

Hans setting all established rules at defiance, and decorating this irregular old house in a way peculiar to his genius. Very interesting is his choice of subjects, which we may divide into the religious and the secular. The former are devoted to the decoration of the room set apart for a chapel. In one beautiful conception we have the fourteen saints (said to have appeared to a shepherd in 1445), kneeling in adoration before the Infant Christ. In another, the family of the donor, husband, wife, and three boys, kneel before seven saints. A third represents a religious procession. By the large open fireplace, Holbein depicted the well-known 'Fountain of Health.' From all sides eager groups approach the large round basin, with its centre column crowned with the arms of the Herstenstein family. Men, women, and children, old and young, hasten to secure the water. The most remarkable figure in the group is that of an old woman, carried in a basket upon her husband's back and holding in her arms a dog, who is also to share the reviving draught. An original sketch of one of the façade paintings is in the Basel Museum. It represents Leæna before her judges, when, rather than speak, she bites off her tongue. A later recollection of Lucerne is found in the Basel Gallery, in the background of a 'Madonna' which presents a distant view of the town with its celebrated bridge.

It has often been questioned whether Hans Holbein ever visited Italy. Van Mander's assertion that he did not, can hardly be accepted as proof. We have evidence in the Basel town records that he more than once obtained permission to visit France, the Netherlands, and England for the sale of his works. There is at least a probability that he may have gone as far as Lombardy and Northern

Italy. Whilst we attribute some of his evident knowledge of the Italian school of painting to the fact that Burckmaer—whose intimacy with the Holbein family we have noticed—had in his employment an Italian artist, this would hardly account for the resemblance some of Holbein's productions bear to the works of Andrea Mantegna. In the same way his acquaintance with the Milanese school would appear likely from his evident acquaintance with the works of Lionardo da Vinci. A 'Last Supper,' painted on wood at Basel, seems to corroborate this opinion. Some inference as to a journey to Italy may be found in the frequent introduction of fig-trees and fig-leaves in his later works, but on the other hand we find surprisingly little of Italian life or landscape.

Soon after his return to Basel Holbein painted the portrait of Bonifacius Amerbach, one of his most perfect works, and in many respects equal to his later pictures in England. Bonifacius was a son of the publisher, Hans Amerbach, and a friend of Erasmus, who finally made him his heir. He must have been well worthy of this friendship, for his moral and intellectual qualities were of the highest order. The noble features, somewhat prominent nose, finely-formed mouth, and bearded chin are given in Holbein's happiest manner. The eyes, partially concealed by the overshadowing brow, beam with intellect and life. A panel at the side of the portrait gives the date 1519, and indicates the time when Amerbach left Freiburg on account of the plague, and settled in Basel. Amerbach's name is still more inseparably connected with the renowned painter on account of the collection in Basel called after him. This collection contains no less than 104 original drawings by Holbein, besides the illustrations of the "Praise of Folly."

Once settled in Basel as a citizen, every year bears witness to Holbein's activity. He is employed in wall-painting, in designing for glass, in drawing for engravers and in the illustration of books. It is difficult to picture Basel as it then appeared, decorated as it was externally by his hand. Some of his wall-paintings remained for a long time: a house at the corner of the Eisengasse was, until the middle of the last century, an excellent specimen of his skill in this particular branch of art. Fortunately we possess etchings and drawings of the greater portion of his designs, which enable us to judge in some measure of the effect produced. When we consider the immense labour bestowed upon this one house, the sum of forty florins, which was all he received for it, seems ridiculously small, even allowing for the greater value of money at that time. In the decoration of the front of this building he introduced an architectural design, and the eye was deceived into supposing that the house itself was handsomely built. The celebrated 'Peasants' Dance' adorned the façade: the dancing figures of men, women, and children keep time to the musicians, who are leaning against a table bearing jugs and glasses. They are drawn with such spirit that their enjoyment seems perfectly real and infectious. Above the second storey large pillars and antique figures of old mythological personages filled in the space, whilst a splendid balustrade appeared to support the third storey and was covered with gaily-dressed figures. Below, on the ground floor, Holbein painted a stable, and by a curious perspective arrangement showed the interior, with a noble steed led by a groom. A column beside the horse was crowned with a figure of Hebe. A water-colour sketch of the 'Peasants' Dance' is extant in the

Basel collection, and there is an undoubted original drawing, touched up with Indian ink, of the same subject in the same Museum. Nowhere has he found a better subject for his pencil than in the spirited and life-like figures of the dancers.

More important, probably, and certainly more lucrative, was a commission to decorate the old Town Hall. This order he received during the mayoralty of Burgomaster Meyer, and, no doubt, through his influence. Unfortunately the greater part of Holbein's work was destroyed by damp and other casualties, but copies still in existence enable us to arrive at a fair estimate of the production. The hall had no architectural beauty, but Holbein by well designed pillars and niches gave it a grand effect. Large historical paintings presented a series of actions, apparently carried on at a distance. Amongst the figures were many of the citizens of the day; and the niches were occupied by figures bearing scrolls, on which were written texts or maxims. Amongst them, 'Justice' with the scales, 'Wisdom' with a double face, and 'Moderation' clad in light garments with bare neck and shoulders, and occupied in pouring wine from a large goblet into a small glass, are conspicuous. We read also of large inscriptions, but no trace of them remains; most likely pictures accompanied them. The council appears to have been satisfied with the painter's work, for we find that the latest payment was made in advance, before the back-wall, as it was called, was even commenced. No doubt the disturbances in Basel and the surrounding country were the reason of the discontinuance of the work, but in spite of these disorders, we have increasing testimony to the activity of Holbein's unflagging industry.

TWO SOLDIERS WITH SHIELD.

A design by Holbein for glass painting, in the Berlin Museum.

His designs for glass paintings were quite original in their treatment: several of them are to be seen in the Basel gallery. Studies from history, coats of arms, fanciful delineations, battle scenes, fruit, flowers, and leaves abound. Noteworthy amongst the larger pieces are the full-length representations of two of the mercenary soldiers of the time, with elaborate surroundings and ornamentations in the renaissance style. Ten sheets give costumes of women, showing with wonderful accuracy the mode of the day. Every detail, from the feathered hat to the graceful folds of the dress, held, according to the fashion, in the right hand, is faithfully delineated.

The 'Peasants' Dance' appears again as a book illustration. It has been used as a border in many publications, as well as the 'Children's Dance.' The immense number of woodcuts known to be by Hans Holbein, makes it quite impossible to name them all. Much discussion has arisen among scientific authorities as to whether Holbein engraved as well as designed his woodcuts; but a thorough investigation of the subject shows clearly that the drawing and the engraving were by entirely different men. No doubt all the more eminent artists knew how to engrave, but they certainly did not, as a usual thing, use the graver. Some of the questions upon this point arose from the confusion of the signatures, and the prevalence of the Christian name Hans added to this confusion. There no longer exists any doubt that the engraver or cutter of Holbein's best designs was Hans Lützelburger, who must have thoroughly understood the engraver's art, or he never could have treated the details and intricacies of his work so well as he did.

A little book of woodcuts, entitled the 'Dance of Death,' or more accurately 'Pictures of Death,' is our best authority

THE KING.

THE QUEEN.

THE PHYSICIAN.

THE ASTROLOGER.

THE KNIGHT.

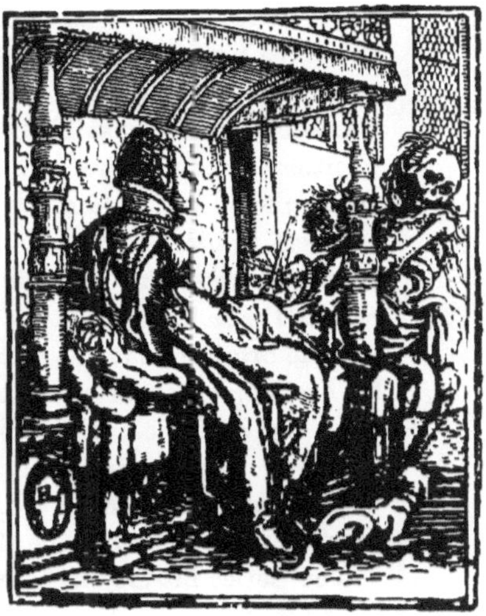

THE DUCHESS.

THE PEDLAR.

THE CHILD.

for the excellence of Hans Lützelburger's interpretation of the artist's meaning. These woodcuts are the most famous of all Holbein's designs, and have an immense reputation. Sandrart relates that Rubens, on his journey to Utrecht, mentioned them to his companions, and advised a youth to study them well, adding, that he himself had made copies of them in his early days. The subject of this renowned series of woodcuts is a very old one. From time immemorial Death had been a favourite theme of representation, but the origin of the so-called 'Dance of Death' is said to be French. It was used to decorate the mortuary of a cemetery in Paris. Holbein, however, treated the subject in a way peculiar to himself; not only illustrating that "in the midst of life we are in death," but also that in every action of our life the thought of death may enter.

The series begins with scenes from the commencement of the world. In the third picture Death, playing a lute, escorts Adam and Eve from Eden. In another, as Adam, by the sweat of his brow, earns his bread, Death assists him in digging up a tree. Now and then we are reminded that the artist has studied old pictures on the subject, but in spite of this, his originality proclaims itself.

Almost every class is represented in this wonderful series. The king at a well-spread board is served by Death, who fills his bowl. Behind the cardinal's chair Death is taking off his hat whilst a petitioner hands him a document with five seals. The queen walking with her ladies is seized by Death dressed as a woman. In a landscape with flocks of sheep, illumined by the western sun. Death terrifies an aged bishop. Here we see Death running away with the abbot's mitre and crozier; there he visits the physician and the astrologer. In the church a hypocritical preacher holds the people in awe, but behind him is a preacher more dread still. Of all in office only one escapes the artist's satire—a parish priest, who administers to a sick member of his flock. Death with bell and lanthorn shows the dying man the way. The miser with his money-bags, the merchant with his bales, are alike surprised by Death; the knight's armour is defenceless; the pedlar with his basket cannot escape; the waggoner's wine-cart is overturned. All are represented in turn: the duchess in her bed; the poor woman in her hovel; the fool who flies in vain; the child who is taken ruthlessly from its mother. Several other subjects were introduced in later issues. In one of these a bride and bridegroom are hurried away by Death. In an edition of 1545 are several additional woodcuts of children at play, and that of 1562 again contains new groups. All are original and all carry out minute details, though we are occasionally reminded in them of the want of anatomical knowledge, a failing common to the artists of the period.

In every edition the series closes with two special cuts. One contains the Last Judgment, in which Christ, sitting on a rainbow, with His feet resting on the world, appears in judgment on the risen figures of saints, who with up-stretched hands are praising God. All appear reconciled, and a peaceful feeling is apparent. Christ alone, in this composition, is partially covered with a mantle, the saints and other figures are without attire. The concluding cut is a curiously arranged shield, bearing the arms of Death. A Death's head, the hour-glass which forms the crest of the helmet, and two dead hands holding stones, occupy the centre. The figure of a man is on one side, of a woman on the other: these are supposed to represent Holbein and his wife.

In connection with these renowned woodcuts, we must refer to the almost equally famous 'Alphabet of Death.' Many of the miniature sketches which it comprises are taken from the larger woodcuts; many again are original. In all we trace Holbein's keen sympathy with the movement of the Reformation. The rich and powerful are invariably depicted as struggling against the "last enemy." The ecclesiastical dignitaries are keenly satirized, whilst the poor, the feeble, and the neglected are tenderly treated. In many of the letters of this alphabet, Holbein introduces two skeletons, symbolic of the double death of body and soul.

We may, perhaps, imagine some sympathy between the treatment of the subject in Holbein's pictures of Death and the circumstances of the time. The Peasants' War in 1514 occasioned immense misery, and succeeding epidemics gave rise to much gloomy feeling. Three more alphabets, perhaps not so well known as that of Death, but still very clever in execution, are also ascribed to Holbein. They are the 'Peasants' Alphabet,' the 'Sport of Infants,' and an ornamental alphabet, consisting of twenty-three letters only.

His illustrations for books are well known; one of his first Basel undertakings was a title-page, which is marked with his abbreviated name, HANS HOLB. It appeared as early as 1516, possibly a year sooner, in works printed by Johann Froben. It represents a niche in the renaissance style; the title is printed on a curtain which falls in front of it. The drawing is exceedingly bold and good, but the cutting is inferior Another title-page has a representation after the style of an altar, in which a train of sea-gods and numbers of little children are depicted. Of the date 1515

is another bearing the initials H. H., having for its subject an incident in ancient history; and another, more elaborate still, gives the "table of Cebes." This is particularly full of human life and humour, and is decorated with the artist's monogram.

In the year 1518 Froben published More's "Utopia," and for that work Hans and his brother Ambrosius designed title-pages, illustrating by their treatment their perfect understanding of the contents of the volume. A large woodcut brings the island of Utopia itself before the reader, in strict accordance with the description given by the author. In addition to these, many learned books, mathematical and astronomical, were illustrated by the brothers.

A grand design forms the opening page of the "Town Laws of Freiburg," with numerous marginal drawings. His 'Peasants' and 'Children's Dances' occur again and again. Many of the printers' devices also owe their origin to him. Amongst them that of Valentin Curio, which contains the "tablet of Parrhasius." Holbein often makes a play upon the name, as in the device of Christopher Froschover of Zurich, for whom he designed a charming little panel, containing a willow-tree over which frogs (*frosch*) are climbing, and for Palma Bebel a renaissance shield with a palm-tree. All are beautifully executed with ornamented accessories.

In the year 1521 the Reformation began to make a stir in Basel, and the following year saw the first issue in that town of Luther's German translation of the New Testament, which had already appeared in Germany. For this edition in folio Holbein designed a magnificent page, in which St. Peter and St. Paul are standing opposite each other: the former, holding a huge key, is absorbed in the book in his hand, the latter holds a sword as well as a book. In the corners are the symbols of the Evangelists, above are the Basel arms, and below, the publisher's device containing the date 1523. In spite of a Brief from the Pope forbidding the issue of Luther's books, a second edition appeared, and this also had a title-page by Holbein. Throughout the volume are illustrations in the text, some of them very beautiful, as well as many large and small initial letters.

We find Hans illustrating for no less than five printers at Basel[1]—Johann Froben, Andreas Cratander, Valentin Curio, Palma Bebel, and Adam Petri,—as well as for Christoph Froschover of Zurich, for all of whom he designed title-pages between 1515 and 1528.

The earliest German copy of the New Testament had scarcely appeared before Adam Petri reprinted it in Basel. For this Holbein designed the initial letters, and many of the woodcuts are evidently by his hand, but the title-page was the work of Urs Graf. A beautiful title-page for Bugenhagen's "Interpretation of the Psalms" is Holbein's, and so is one to a work by Miconius published in Zürich, in 1528. Again, we find a drawing of the 'Feeding of the five thousand;' and a decorative title-page engraved on metal in 1528 bears his initials. Two large woodcuts, which appear to have been published alone, are his; one, 'The Saviour bearing His Cross,' appears a solitary figure without any of the usual accessories. Our Lord, beneath the terrible weight of the Cross, has fallen upon His knees; supported by His right hand, He tries to rise; His

[1] In "Die Bücher-ornamentik der Renaissance," by A. F. Butsch, recently published, there are twenty-four plates of title-pages and ornaments by Hans Holbein and his brother Ambrosius.

left hand grasps the cross-beam of His burden; the crown of thorns pierces His brow. The deepest suffering is here portrayed: the mouth, open as if to cry aloud, yet refraining to utter a sound; the beseeching eyes, and the attitude of the almost quivering figure, all denote the anguish of the Lord.

A woodcut giving the 'Resurrection of Christ,' comprised of eight distinct sheets, is to be met with at Gotha, and is catalogued as Holbein's work; but probably only a small design was really drawn by him.

A series of woodcuts from the Old Testament history must have been first designed about this time, although the first printed edition did not come out till 1538. There is no doubt that they appeared with the first movement of the Reformation. They began with the extremely rare 'Fall of Man,' afterwards published in the Latin Bible at Lyons, but which is missing in most of the first issues of the woodcuts. Many of these cuts were undoubtedly engraved by Lützelburger, and, after his death, by less able hands. Holbein appears to have been particularly at home in the subjects of the Old Testament, and treated them with great vigour and reality. His figures are all real men and women, somewhat too broad perhaps in person, but dramatically conceived. He contents himself with depicting the natural, and does not introduce any supernatural accessories. His woodcuts appealed to the spirit of the age, and were eagerly seized upon; so much so, that we find orders in council prohibiting the publication of any works not previously examined by the magistrates. Two compositions especially attracted their notice; they were in the very spirit of Luther; the one depicted the 'Sale of Indulgences,' the other, 'Christ as the True Light.' In the latter, the

THE HAPPINESS OF THE GODLY.—*Psalm* i. 1.

DESTRUCTION OF THE ASSYRIAN HOST.—2 *Chron.* xxxii. 21.

JOAB'S ARTIFICE.—2 *Samuel* xiv. 4.

ESTHER CROWNED QUEEN.—*Esther* ii. 17.

peasants and the unlearned are represented following the Saviour, while the churchmen and learned turn their backs upon Him scornfully. We find the same influence in a woodcut in the Erlangen collection, which represents the Pope in the midst of a stately procession, whilst the Saviour approaches him on a donkey, followed by His Apostles. A date given on the Pope's letter shows this to be a production of 1524.

One of Holbein's most realistic paintings is a picture of the dead Christ. It is labelled as being intended for the Saviour, otherwise the want of the devotional element in its treatment would have suggested it as intended simply for one who had died a violent death. The absence of colour, and the livid hue of the outstretched corpse upon the green stone coffin lend a terror to the picture which is startlingly effective.[1] On this one occasion Holbein allowed himself full latitude in depicting the horrors of death. We find much of the same feeling but less vivid in two companion paintings for panels, of the 'Man of Sorrows,' and the Virgin, who is represented as the 'Mother of Sorrows.' The Saviour is represented seated, His brow encircled with a crown of thorns; His mother kneels with outstretched hands. Both are printed in subdued yellow tints, with white lights in a blue atmosphere, and are very fine in effect. We notice the same absence of colour in the paintings on the organ-doors in Basel cathedral, which, escaping the iconoclastic storm, remained in their places until a new organ was lately introduced; they were then removed to the Public Art Collection, where they may now be seen at the entrance of the Museum. In these paintings, the patron Saints of the

---

[1] This has lately been engraved in "Hans Holbein," by Paul Mantz.

cathedral occupy the opposite corners of the right wing; the Virgin, holding in her arms the clinging Child, stands to the right; to the left, the Emperor Maximilian, in his royal mantle, gazes intently on the crucifix, while in the distance behind him appears his consort Kunigund; between them we see the buildings of the choir. The corresponding wing gives us St. Pantalus, first Bishop of Basel, with the crozier; groups of angels, singing and making music, fill up the space between him and the Madonna. Every part of the painting is full of figures of angels, some are blowing trumpets, others sing round a scroll of music; the very air seems full of harmony. Different ornamental designs decorate the opposite pictures—leaves, scrolls, and architectural ornaments.

In Freiburg Cathedral are two altar panels by Holbein, which show a marvellous effect of light. They represent respectively the 'Holy Birth,' and the 'Adoration of the Magi.' Holbein conceives the subject in the spirit of the apocryphal gospel, which tells how at the birth the whole cave was filled with glorious light, and he manages the effect so wonderfully, that the glory emanating from the child touches with beautiful sheen the bending head of the Virgin. Below these panels are representations of the donor's family. On the one side stands the father supported by his sons, on the other the mother with her daughters. On the one panel we find the arms of the Oberriedt family, on the other those of the Zscheckapürlins, and this enables us to trace the origin of the pictures. Councillor Oberriedt was a native of Basel; he is mentioned in connection with Holbein in 1521, when a sum of money owing to the painter was made over to the councillor, probably in payment of a debt.

In all likelihood, these panels were in the first instance intended for some Basel church, and were sent for safe keeping to Freiburg during the disturbances between Church and State.

In the Kunsthalle at Carlsruhe there are two pictures conceived in much the same spirit: one represents St. Ursula with the arrow, the other St. George with the dragon. The former is dated 1522. These also were evidently intended for altar-panels, but are very unequal in execution. Whilst the face and bust of St. Ursula are in Holbein's happiest manner, the lower part of the figure and that of St. George are so inferior as to suggest a less skilful hand. Probably designed, and in part painted, by the master himself, they were executed under his direction, but without very careful supervision.

CHAPTER III.

The Solothurn and the Meyer Madonna—Portraits of Melancthon and Erasmus—Letter of Erasmus to Sir Thomas More—Disturbances at Basel—Contemplated Journey to England.

1522 TO 1526.

OF all Holbein's sacred pictures, none are more justly celebrated than the two called the 'Solothurn Madonna' and the 'Meyer Madonna.' The former has only lately become known; it was probably painted for the Cathedral of Solothurn, and afterwards removed to the little village church of Grenchen. This picture is highly finished, but it suffered slightly in its restoration in 1867. In the centre, the Madonna, with an expression of heavenly love and peace, holds the Holy Infant in her lap; the Child is charmingly painted, the outward turn of the hand and the wrinkle in the chubby little foot are true to nature. The Madonna is represented with her neck bare, in a light red dress; over it she wears a very amply-folded mantle of ultramarine blue. The carpet on the steps at her feet has a green ground crossed with red and white lines; her mantle sweeps the steps, and partially covers the arms that are woven into the pattern of the carpet. On her left hand is St. Ursus, patron Saint of Solothurn, and on her right, Martin, Bishop of Tours. It has been suggested with great plausibility that Holbein found his model for both the Madonna and the Child in his own family. We have no exact account of his marriage, but in the will of his uncle Sigismund Holbein, mention is made of Hans' wife Elspeth, and a later notice of her speaks of her son Franz Schmid. It seems clear, therefore, that Holbein married a widow, and more than probable that the infant here depicted was his first child. We are confirmed in this idea by reference to some sketches in silver pencil in the Weigel collection of a mother and child, which give the same features, and bear the same date, 1522, as the Solothurn painting. And again, a later painting by Holbein of his wife and children, dated 1529, gives the same features in profile, although the child of course is much older. Although this picture of Holbein's wife is far from prepossessing, we must remember that it was taken in a time of trouble, and that she had probably greatly changed since her marriage.

There is in the Louvre a little pencil sketch, touched up with Indian ink and red chalk, unmistakably by Holbein, which depicts his wife as a young and pleasing woman. This drawing represents her with great exactness, but without the idealized expression of the painting. We find precisely the same rather feebly opened eyes, heavy eyelids, large nose, and well-cut mouth, with the same strongly developed chin. The hair in the sketch hangs down in two long braids, and the shoulders and neck are broad and uncovered. A necklace, the same as that given to St. Ursula at Carlsruhe, is round the neck, whilst embroidered on her dress, is the constantly recurring device ALS IN ERN. She appears as a strong, healthy, pleasing girl of the people, with a smile, which, if not very intelligent, is bright and pleasant. Strongly as Holbein's genius has

idealized her in the 'Solothurn Madonna,' the individuality is still easily perceived. And she is seen, though not quite so plainly, in his world-renowned master-piece at Darmstadt.

The 'Meyer Madonna' has given rise to more discussion than any known work. There are two versions of it, each claiming to be the original, and until the Dresden Exhibition of 1871 allowed the two paintings to be examined side by side, art critics found it quite impossible to arrive at any conclusion. Once, however, brought face to face, not only with the two pictures but with such a number of Holbein's works as enabled a thorough comparison to be made, no doubt remained in any mind capable of judging that the great master's handiwork was to be found in the Darmstadt picture, and that the Dresden Madonna was the work of a painter of a later period. It is impossible to go over every inch of ground which the various art authorities fought out amongst themselves; we must be content with the result arrived at. It was shown by careful comparison of details, that the Darmstadt Madonna only was the positive creation and production of Hans Holbein. With this then alone we have to do, merely noticing, in passing, that the painter of the Dresden 'Meyer Madonna,' unknown as he still remains, was second only in genius to the great master himself.

According to the fashion we so constantly find in the paintings of that period, the donor of this famous picture is represented in it, not however in the usual subordinate position, but most conspicuously kneeling with all his family in adoration of the Holy Mother and Child. There is no limit to the suggestions which this creation of Holbein's genius has occasioned. At one time it was supposed that the child in Mary's arms was a sick member of the family, and that the little naked boy, beside the son of the Burgomaster, was intended for the Infant Christ. Another authority thought, that while the child in the Virgin's arms represented the sufferer, the boy who is standing was the same after recovery. It is needless to state that there never was sufficient ground for any of these hypotheses. Holbein was the last man in the world to introduce an obscure meaning into his pictures, and the earliest records of this particular altar-piece invariably mention it as 'Maria with the Holy Child,' or 'Maria with the Infant Christ.'

In this picture, as in the 'Solothurn Madonna,' the Virgin occupies the central position, somewhat raised above the kneeling figures. She holds the infant in a caressing manner, its little head nestling in her neck, and looks down on the worshipping family with beaming tenderness and love. On her right the Burgomaster Meyer of Hasen, already familiar to us from Holbein's early portrait, kneels in rapt adoration, with his clasped hands upon the shoulder of his son, beside whom stands the naked boy who has given rise to so much imaginative speculation. On the opposite side we have three female figures; the one nearest to the Virgin Mother, with her head wrapped in linen, is supposed to represent the Burgomaster's deceased wife, whilst the figure below her is sufficiently like the young wife we have already mentioned, to be recognized as Dorothea Kannegiesser. By her side we find the daughter with her rosary. The marvellous conception of this picture is seen above all in the ordinary accessories of the scene. The Virgin is shown in familiar proximity to the family, almost as one of them; her elevation alone shows that she extends to them, as it were, the mantle of grace.

Resting on the shoulder of the kneeling Burgomaster, the mantle also shields the adoring women.[1] The treatment of the subject and all the accessories are entirely original; we see in them no trace of the earlier masters, unless, perhaps, the foliage of the fig-tree may suggest some little acquaintance with Italian art.

Two pictures in the Basel Museum, which betray foreign influence, are undoubtedly the work of Hans Holbein. They are two distinct representations of the same beautiful young woman: in the one, Cupid with his arrows proclaims her the Goddess of Love; in the other she is inscribed, after a celebrated courtesan, LAIS CORINTHIACA. Some hidden meaning has been suggested for the strangely satirical significance of this superscription, but nothing certain is known of the original, although, as the pictures are catalogued by Amerbach as "two tablets upon which an Offenburgin is delineated," it is supposed that she belonged to the Offenburg family. In them we trace more decidedly than in most of Holbein's works the influence of the Lombard school.

But marvellous as Holbein's paintings were, it is sufficiently evident that it was his skill as a portrait painter which rendered him most famous in his day. The disturbances at Basel, the troubles and uncertainties of the Council, perhaps, had something to do with the comparatively small number of paintings from his easel which dealt with miscellaneous subjects; but it is quite clear that he was widely employed in painting portraits.

In the Welfen Museum in Hanover is a small circular

---

[1] There are slight differences in the details of the Darmstadt and the Dresden pictures.

portrait of Melancthon; it is certainly the best likeness we possess of the Reformer; the contour of the head is particularly fine. It was formerly in a case, on the border of which were graceful renaissance ornaments and figures of satyrs. An inscription on the frame, bearing testimony to Holbein's skill, is probably the tribute offered to the artist by Melancthon himself.

We have seen how thoroughly Holbein appreciated and understood the humour of Erasmus in his illustrations of the 'Praise of Folly,' and further evidence of his acquaintance with the scholar exists in his many portraits of that great man. The earliest of them is that now in the possession of the Earl of Radnor, at Longford Castle, which was once supposed to be by Quentin Matsys. On examination, it is clear that the portrait which Erasmus described in a letter which he wrote to Sir Thomas More, as having been painted by Matsys, was in no particular like the one now mentioned. The picture at Longford Castle is thoroughly in Holbein's style, and is a counterpart, in many respects, of Holbein's drawings at Paris.

The portrait of Erasmus belonging to Lord Radnor is therefore clearly to be attributed to Holbein. The great commentator, whose hair is already grey, wears a fur coat and a doctor's hat. The face is taken at three-quarters and turns to the left; the background is in the renaissance style, with a green curtain half concealing a shelf with books, admitting us, as it were, into the privacy of the student. The hands, treated with Holbein's peculiar delicacy, rest on a book which is inscribed "ΗΡΑΚΛΕΙΟΙ ΠΟΝΟΙ ERASMI," "the Herculean labours of Erasmus."

A second portrait of the same date (1523) is in the Louvre. It is painted in warmer colours than the last

named, and represents Erasmus in profile, the silvery
hair peeping beneath his scholar's cap; again the background is a green curtain, this time covered with a pattern. The inscription on the Louvre picture is no longer
discernible, but on a portrait of the same period at Basel,
we can distinctly read the words Erasmus is writing. His
delicately formed hands rest upon the manuscript upon
his desk, and with the right he points with the pen to the
words

> " In Evangelum Marci paraphrasis per
> D. Erasmum Roterodamium aucto (rem)
> Cunctis mortalibus ins (itum est),"

forming the beginning of his paraphrase of St. Mark,
which appeared in 1523. Many copies of these familiar
pictures are ascribed to Holbein, which are certainly not
his work, though doubtless he produced more than one
repetition himself, and many others may have proceeded
from his studio. A small circular portrait of the great
scholar in the Basel collection is excellent, but as he
appears somewhat older, it was probably executed at a
later period. Erasmus, in a letter to Pirkheimer, mentions
that he sent two pictures of himself to London : one,
intended for Warham, Archbishop of Canterbury, whom
Erasmus was in the habit of calling his Maecenas, and to
whom he was indebted for many kindnesses, is identified
with the picture now at Longford Castle, but it is impossible to tell what became of the other. Perhaps Sir
Thomas More received one, but in writing to Erasmus, although he extols the painter highly, he does not thank the
sender of the picture mentioned in his letter as if it were
a gift to himself. Erasmus also notices a portrait, sent

by him to France, under charge of the painter himself, which was most likely intended for his great friend Amer-

HANS HOLBEIN. *From the drawing by himself at Basel.*

bach, then staying at Avignon, but we have no certain record of this fact.

Before we close our notice of the paintings and sketches

belonging to the time of Holbein's lengthened stay in Basel, we must not forget to mention the portrait of himself, to which we are indebted for our ideas of him in his early manhood. This is a slight sketch, now in the Basel Museum. It is called in the Amerbach catalogue "A portrait of Holbein in dry colours." There is a similarity in the features to the early picture of his boyhood, in the Basilica of St. Paul, and in the sketch of him at the age of fourteen. Clean shaven, his face looks that of a man of twenty-four or twenty-five. His nut-brown hair is smooth and short, partially covered with his painter's hat, which slightly shades the forehead. The expression of his countenance is intellectual in the highest degree, the eyes bright and full, the brow fine, broad, and open in expression; whilst a certain curve of the lips gives a slightly ironical appearance to the lower part of the face. The ease of the figure is wonderfully represented.

As we have already intimated, Holbein's fame as a portrait painter had spread far and wide. We find frequent mention of it in the letters which constantly passed between Erasmus and Sir Thomas More; and a German authority states, that long before Holbein finally started upon his journey to London, the Earl of Arundel, when on a visit to Basel as Ambassador, had urged him to try his fortunes in England. This may have been the case, but it seems more credible that he was induced to take this step at the recommendation of Erasmus. The great writer was very well known and much esteemed in England: he was a favourite with King Henry VIII., and was in constant communication with him. Erasmus, whose early life had been sad and careworn, was indebted to England for many happy years, and although we have no direct evidence of the fact, we may surely judge that his encouragement and advice had their due weight in inducing the painter to seek better fortunes for himself.

We have shown how freely Erasmus corresponded with Sir Thomas More; and in a letter dated 1524, intimating to him his intention of sending two portraits to England, Erasmus speaks of the painter's proposed journey thither, and recommends him to the care of his friend. The original letter is lost, but we gather this from Sir Thomas More's reply, which is extant. It is dated the 18th of December, 1525, and in it, before closing, he says, "Thy painter, dearest Erasmus, is a wonderful artist, but I fear he will not find England so fruitful as he hopes." For some reason, however, with which we are not acquainted, the painter's journey was not undertaken until somewhat later. Iselin, in his records, states that Holbein set out upon his journey in the autumn of 1526. Besides the inducement of the gifted Erasmus's recommendation, we can easily imagine that there was much in the position of affairs in Basel to tempt him to leave it. We have already alluded to the troublous times, and before leaving that town with Holbein we may well glance slightly at the events of the period.

In 1526 the Reformation had already made progress: an edict had been issued allowing nuns to marry; public disputations were permitted, and the offices of the Church were conducted in the German language. In spite of the continued opposition of the nobles, privilege after privilege was wrested from them and from the patrons of the Church, whilst freedom of religious opinion gained the upper hand. When speaking of the paintings for the Town-hall, we recorded their discontinuance on account of the disturbances: these increased in number and violence; all business was interrupted, and but little opportunity was afforded for the encouragement of the fine arts. The only entry made by the Council in Holbein's favour during the later years of his stay in the city is sad enough. It is a notice of the payment to him of a small sum of money, equivalent to about four shillings, for a coat-of-arms, painted for a neighbouring village. Whilst in Italy painters were treated and paid as princes, in Germany and Switzerland, owing to the distractions of the time, they could barely earn their bread.

But the unfortunate population of Basel had to endure miseries other than those of internal dissension. In 1526, from spring to autumn, the plague raged with unceasing violence. The people, as usual, attributed it to the anger of God, and their superstitious fears were increased when, in September, a fearful hailstorm occurred, during which the lightning struck a powder magazine; the explosion shook the city, destroying many houses, and more than forty persons were killed or wounded. The distress of the painters is painfully shown in an appeal made by their guild to the Council, that they might retain the monopoly of devising the false beards required for the Carnivals, stating that so many painters had already been obliged to take to other businesses, that the city would soon be unable to boast of any artists at all.

Thus everything worked together in bringing about that journey of Hans Holbein to England, which we may regard as a great event in the history of English art; for undoubtedly to the great German painter we owe the progress made in succeeding years. We have no accurate data of the exact time at which Holbein landed on our coast, but we know he was in England in 1527; and a letter from

Erasmus, dated August 29th, 1526, commends the traveller to his friend Aegidius in Antwerp. Thus we may make sure that his journey took place at the end of the summer, or beginning of the early autumn of that year. Erasmus showed his friendly feeling for Holbein by requesting Aegidius to introduce him, if not personally at least by letter, to his famous contemporary Quentin Matsys, and a sentence at the close of the introduction proves also his entire confidence in the painter, for he says, "You can give him what letters you have." This coming from Erasmus is emphatic, for in his epistles he constantly complains of the untrustworthiness of his messengers. We can imagine that the painter, who had evidently vainly struggled to support himself and family in his adopted country, set out for England with renewed hope and confident of success.

A journey in those days was a very ordinary event. It is hard to conceive the great inducement which so often overcame the difficulties, which we in our enlightened days should think insuperable. Everybody that could do so travelled. The higher classes journeyed on horseback, putting up at the inns and hostelries which romances made famous; but by far the larger number went on foot, taking such rest as they could find at the cheaper inns or halting-places of their particular class. Every artisan or artist wishing for success sought travelling experience. Hans most probably commenced his journey on foot; certainly he was not in circumstances to afford a horse, though it is possible that he may have served in the capacity of messenger for Erasmus, in which case the scholar would, in accordance with the custom of the day, provide for the artist's necessary expenses. We hear a great deal of his difficulty in finding a *famulus*, as he styled

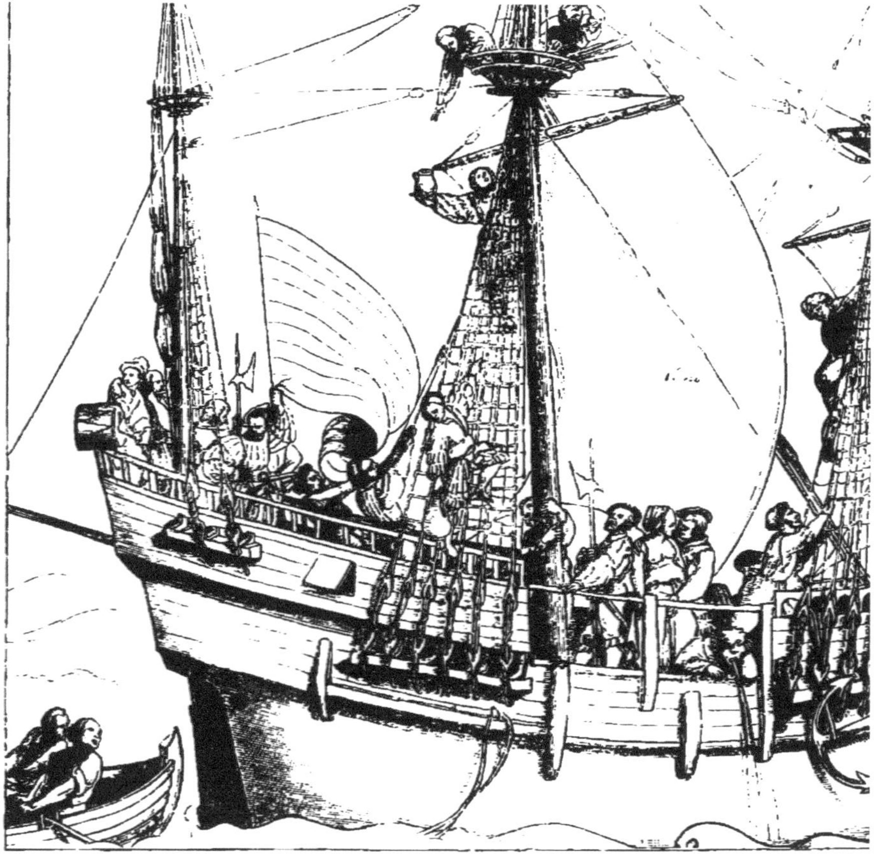

GERMAN SHIP OF THE XVI. CENTURY. *From a drawing by Holbein, i*

a messenger. He most probably confided to Holbein private letters as well as the pictures he mentions.

The most dreaded part of the enterprise was the crossing from Calais to Dover. We do not know how long Holbein took to complete his journey; nor whether he made any prolonged stay in Antwerp, or elsewhere, with the object of earning money. It is possible that we may take a very beautiful drawing of his, now in the Städel Museum at Frankfort, as some evidence that he did. This represents a three-decked vessel on the point of starting. At the stern is a small boat with two rowers: on the deck of the larger vessel all seems in motion; sailors climb up the rigging and unfurl the sails; one salutes a girl, one drinks to a prosperous voyage, while another already succumbs to the dreaded sea-sickness. Two musicians give the signal for departure, and near them we find one of Holbein's masterly delineations of a warrior.

THE FOX-CHASE.

CHAPTER IV.

Holbein's first Visit to London—Sir Thomas More's house and family—Portraits of More, Archbishop Warham, and Bishop Fisher—Other portraits.

1527 TO 1528.

HOLBEIN arrived in London in the 18th year of Henry VIII.'s reign, at a time when the king's popularity was unbounded and the troubles of the future were little anticipated. The king's love of learning and the encouragement given both by himself and his learned consort, Katharine of Arragon, to the fine arts, drew to his Court the best ability of the age. His handsome person and cheerful manners made him much beloved, and his popularity was heightened by his love of show, which led to many noble pageants and to a constant succession of exciting entertainments and amusements. The higher classes of England at this time were distinguished by their refinement and learning, in great contrast to the coarseness and ignorance of the common people. The nobility followed Henry's example of collecting works of art, and it is said that the king never allowed the key of his gallery out of his possession. But although Holbein's introduction to Sir Thomas More must have brought him into intimate connection with the Court, he does not appear to have executed any painting specially for the king until ten years after his first arrival. The English Court-painter of the day was one John Browne; but no doubt there were other English favourites, beside many foreigners, especially Italians and Flemings. Of these Toto and Penni are often mentioned in the Royal Household accounts, and so is also Lucas Horebout, a Dutch painter, who was naturalized in 1534. He was the best paid artist of the day, for we find that his yearly salary amounted to £33 6*s.*, whereas Holbein, when in the Royal Household, received only £30 per annum. But if these and other artists rivalled him at first and delayed his success, few of them are remembered, whilst certainly much that never emanated from his studio is attributed to Holbein. To such an extent is this the case, that even now it is very difficult to select from the many pictures imputed to him those which are undoubtedly genuine; and these unfortunately are scattered far and wide, and can only be classified with infinite difficulty. Many which could not by any possibility have been painted till after his death have been catalogued as his; whilst others, which he unquestionably painted, have been lost.

In order to gain an insight into Holbein's wonderful industry upon his first coming to England, we must refer to the drawings, the property of the Queen, in Windsor Castle. There are eighty-seven portraits drawn on tinted paper with coloured chalks; the effect in many cases being heightened by shading in Indian ink. Many of these sketches are as large as life and some are covered with pin-pricks, proving them to have been used for tracing. The names inscribed cannot, in every instance, be relied upon, as they were catalogued at a later period. The collection formerly contained more sketches than it does at present, some of them having been removed. The entire series was at one time in the possession of the Earl of Arundel, and appears to have been completely forgotten, until Queen Caroline, the wife of George II., found them hidden away in a cupboard in Kensington Palace. They were then carefully framed, and afterwards were removed to Windsor and re-mounted. In 1792 Chamberlain published a series of engravings from them, but, with the exception of two or three, the copies were unequal and weak. During the last few years, the Science and Art Department have published a set of autotypes in red pigment,[1] taken direct from the drawings, which give us an admirable idea of the original works.

Holbein could have had no better introduction when he arrived in England than that to Sir Thomas More. This accomplished man was not only constantly employed as an Ambassador, but was Chancellor of the Exchequer, and Member of the Privy Council. Holbein's name must have been very familiar to him, not only through Erasmus but also through Froben, and as the author of the charming illustrations to the "Utopia." At this time More lived at Chelsea, or rather his country-house was there; and there he welcomed the foreign and friendless artist. Letters of Erasmus make us familiar with More's house and mode of living. Many happy days had the scholar passed under its hospitable roof. More, distinguished as a courtier, was not less valued at home: Erasmus relates that, however wearied he was, upon his return from his professional duties or the State cares which demanded his attention, he always found time to interest himself in his

[1] These may be seen at the South Kensington Museum.

home life. One of his favourite maxims was that every one ought to be as agreeable towards others as possible. King Henry valued his counsels, and often sent for him to consult with him privately on affairs of State, or to discuss difficult and abstruse questions with him. More than once Henry visited him in his own home, and on some such occasion may have heard of Holbein, if he did not actually meet him. Erasmus compared More's family life to a second Republic of Plato, but added "that is too small a comparison, with more justice we might call this house a school of Christian feeling." Evidence of the purity of Holbein's life and conduct is found in his admission to such a household, and he probably sympathized with the family in all their pursuits and studies, with the one exception of their religious exercises. More was a staunch Roman Catholic, and Holbein must have been forced to conceal his predilections for the doctrines of the Reformation.

The natural thing for More to do upon receiving his talented guest was to give him a commission. Probably the portrait dated MDXXVII. was the painter's first work in England. It was sent by Mr. Henry Huth to the National Historical Portrait Exhibition, held at South Kensington in the year 1866, and was then considered, although it had evidently been retouched, one of the best of Holbein's works. It gives a representation of More's half-length figure, life-size, in dark green coat with fur collar and crimson sleeves, the hands resting lightly together, the right holding a paper, the arms leaning against a table on which the date is given; the Chancellor is looking to the right; a heavy golden chain is round his neck with double roses as ornaments. The green curtain in the background has a red cord, and on the one side we catch a glimpse of the blue sky. More was at this time clean shaven, but we know that in later years he wore a beard, for when he laid his head upon the block, it is recorded that he held his beard on one side, saying, "This has committed no treason." Erasmus' early description of More as a handsome youth is fully borne out by this painting, and while his face shows the repose of a cultivated mind, it also exhibits the gravity which is the result of a full acquaintance with the cares of life.

Many so-called portraits of More have been erroneously attributed to Holbein, amongst them one of a bearded man with a little dog, in the Brussels Gallery, which was engraved by Vorsterman in 1631. No doubt remains that it was the work of a French artist. On the other hand, there is a beautiful work by Holbein in the Louvre; but then it is not a portrait of More at all, but of Sir Thomas Wyat of Allington Castle, a statesman of the time of Henry VII., and a member of Henry VIII.'s Privy Council. The mistake of cataloguing it as a likeness of More probably arose from the heavy gold chain he wears. Wyat's strong and impressive face bears no resemblance to the Chancellor's refined features. In the Windsor collection of drawings there is a portrait of Wyat, and there are two genuine portraits of More, but they are much damaged.

It would be difficult to find a more graphic and life-like picture than that of Warham, Archbishop of Canterbury. In the Windsor collection his strongly-marked features are vividly given; the drawing is touched with a masterly hand. A finished painting after the sketch is to be found in Lambeth Palace: it is a half-length picture, and the firm strong hands rest on the gold brocaded cushion; an open book and a large jewelled cross give

ARCHBISHOP WARHAM.

From the painting by Holbein, in the Louvre.

importance to the picture. The details of the cross recall Van Eyck in the minuteness of the workmanship. In the Louvre is a second copy, undoubtedly by the master himself, which is more harmonious than the original in Lambeth Palace, but which from its cold grey tint appears a little hard. The old man, born in 1456, already bent with age, is represented with all his earnestness of expression. These different studies of him were most likely made in 1527, for as the friend of Erasmus, the archbishop would naturally have interested himself in the painter.

Probably it was about this time that Holbein drew the portrait of another friend and patron of Erasmus, Fisher, Bishop of Rochester, of whom we find two sketches, one in the Windsor collection, and the other in the British Museum. No finished painting from them is in existence; the face, with its honest and modest expression, yet worn and anxious, suggests the character of the man whom Erasmus so highly extolled for his purity of life and kindness to all with whom he came into contact.

Sir Henry Guildford, Master of the Horse, another intimate friend of Sir Thomas More, was painted in the same year. He was a soldier and a scholar. In his picture he holds the staff of office as Lord Treasurer, and wears the collar of the Order of the Garter. His dress is figured with gold, and his black overcoat is trimmed with sable. The yellow colour of his complexion was peculiar to him, and occurs in the sketch as well as in the painting. At the time the likeness was taken he was forty-nine years of age. Lady Guildford's portrait was formerly in the collection of the Duke of Buckingham at Stowe; it was exhibited in the National Historical Portrait Exhibition of 1868 by Mr. T. Frewen.

One more portrait belonging to Holbein's first year in England is in the Dresden Gallery; it represents a man in a fur-trimmed cap and coat; a paper which he holds in his hand gives the date.

In the following year Holbein was better known. We find him painting the portrait of King Henry VIII.'s astronomer, Nicolas Kratzer, now in the Louvre. Kratzer is drawn as large as life, and turns to the right, as usual in Holbein's pictures, in full light. A brown upper garment covers his black coat, the edge of a red waistcoat appears at the back of the neck. Mathematical instruments hang on the wall or lie on the table, and a sheet of paper bears Kratzer's name and the date 1528. The face is beardless, and though not exactly beautiful, is very striking: a somewhat heavy figure, yet very full of character, gives a vivid impression of him.

A small portrait of Thomas Godsalve of Norwich and his son, sitting together at a table, has the date 1528 on the wall. They are so much alike that the relationship is unquestionable. A second portrait of the son by Holbein is among the Windsor pictures; it is completely executed in body colours, and is the gem of the collection. He wears a violet coat, which, thrown open, shows the white shirt, and over all is a garment trimmed with fur; the ground is azure blue. The young man has a very puritanical expression, rather borne out by a record in the account book of the Royal household, that in the year 1538, when every one at Court presented a gift to the king, he gave a New Testament.

Among the pictures of this date we may safely name the portrait of Sir Bryan Tuke in the Pinakothek in Munich. He was the Treasurer of the King's household; he died in 1545. The head is covered with a cap, passing over the ears, a fashion of the day; his upper and under garments are trimmed with fur, and the latter also with gold buttons. The usual green curtain forms the background, and a skeleton behind it exhibits an hour-glass. The name of the painter is written on it in the Augsburg orthography IO. HOLPAIN; this picture, although it has suffered in cleaning, is undoubtedly a genuine Holbein. A second picture of the same nobleman is in the possession of the Duke of Westminster. It is in all respects like that at Munich but for the absence of the skeleton, and belongs to the same year. It is signed "BRIANUS TUKE, MILES, Anno Aetatis suæ LVII."

In the Windsor collection there is the portrait of Sir Thomas Elyot, who died in 1546. He was an intimate friend of Erasmus, educated for the law, and a well-known writer of the day. The king valued him for his acquirements, and made him ambassador to the Court of Charles V. A portrait of his wife, Lady Elyot, who afterwards married Sir James Dyer, is the companion drawing.

As an example of Holbein's strict adherence to realism in his earlier English portraits, we may instance one in the Madrid Gallery. It is of a middle-aged man, with little beard, large nose, and plain features. The portrait is of a reddish-brown colour, and the personal appearance of the subject is far from attractive.

CHAPTER V.

The family of Sir Thomas More—Holbein's visit to Basel—His wife and children—Decorates the Town Hall—Returns to England—Merchants of the Steelyard—Marriage of Henry VIII. to Anne Boleyn—Portraits of the English nobility.

1528 TO 1533.

WHETHER Holbein lived constantly in Sir Thomas More's house during all the years of his first visit to London, or not, we have no direct evidence. In 1528 he painted a large picture of 'The Family of Sir Thomas More.' The original is now lost; but Karel van Mander, (who wrote in 1608) mentions it as being then in the possession of the art collector Andries de Loo, from whom it went back to a grandson of Sir Thomas More: since then it has entirely disappeared. Fortunately, however, we find the original sketch in the Basel Museum: it had been sent by More to his old friend Erasmus upon Holbein's return to Basel in the following year. In this sketch we see the family assembled in a simply furnished apartment, probably the dining-hall, for on the left is a buffet covered with tankards, vases, goblets, and bottles—most probably, from their shape, silver—whilst the window-sill is furnished with similar objects. In the centre of the picture we see Sir Thomas More himself; his hands, which we know from historical records were of awkward shape, are dexterously covered with the long sleeves: at his right sits his aged father, Sir John More, whom Sir Thomas tended with affectionate and grateful care. Beside him is a relative of the family, Margaret Gigs, with a book in her hand, apparently pointing out to the old man something she has just read; she is twenty-two years of age. Next in order is Elizabeth Dancy, More's second daughter, drawing on a glove. In the foreground on his left, two other daughters are seated, one of whom is Margaret Roper, her father's favourite, whom he usually called "Meg." She was a most devoted child, and was considered very beautiful. In her father's later and unhappy years, when misfortunes pressed heavily upon him, it was she who visited him in the Tower, and who was with him on his final journey to the scaffold. She holds an open book in her hand. The youngest sister, Cicely (Cecilia, the wife of Giles Heron), half turns towards her stepmother (Alice, Lady More), who is kneeling on a prie-dieu behind the daughters. She has been described by Erasmus as a "too lively little woman:" neither young nor handsome, she was a widow, seven years older than himself, when More married her. She was, however, acknowledged even by Erasmus to be a careful housekeeper and a tender mother. A chained monkey near her reminds us of More's known predilection for pet animals. Close to his father we find John the son in whose scientific advancement More took so great an interest, but who, from the entire absence of all record concerning him, would appear to have possessed very little force of character: he is delineated as a gentle, pleasing youth. Among

THE FAMILY OF SIR THOMAS MORE. *From the sketch at Basel*

the group we find that important member of a household of rank in those days, the family jester (Henry Pattison), a man of forty years of age, a rude jovial fellow in outward appearance. Behind him, in perspective, we catch a glimpse of servants or secretaries reading or writing at the open window. We find no sketch of any of More's sons-in-law, but John's sweetheart, Anne Crisacre, a young girl of about fifteen years of age, with a somewhat haughty and supercilious expression, is standing not by her lover, but rather behind his grandfather, and appears to survey the family group as though hardly sympathizing in all their feelings.

The names of the different members of the group and their ages are written by More himself, but in addition to these, the original drawing has many comments in Holbein's handwriting: for example, over the stepmother's head is written "*Diese soll sitzen*" (this one shall sit), and above Sir John More's head, where a violin and a clock are hanging on the wall, we find a note, "*Klavikordi vnd ander sêyten spill uf ein bretz*" (Clavicords and other instruments on a shelf). We know that the whole family were accomplished musicians, and that even Mistress Alice, to please her husband, had been induced in her old age to learn many instruments.

This valuable drawing gives only the first faint outlines of the intended painting, yet every trait is completely delineated. We see this even moro decidedly when we compare the heads in the Windsor collection, which were evidently taken from life. Various copies of this family picture are to be found in England, mostly of somewhat later date. Of these one copy only, which was long supposed to be the original, is worthy of notice. It is now in the possession of Mr. Winn at his country seat of

Nostell Priory, in Yorkshire. Although this is clearly only a copy, it is an exceedingly able one, and is noteworthy from the fact, that the alterations suggested by the artist in his first rough sketch are carried out. Mistress Alice is sitting, and on the wall are the instruments mentioned. Many of the titles of the books can be plainly read, for instance, in the one Margaret Roper has on her lap is written "L., An. Seneca—Œdipus."

Sir Thomas More sent the original sketch to Erasmus by the painter's own hands; and we find that Holbein must have returned to Basel in the year 1528—instead of 1529, as has been generally supposed—for on the 29th of August in 1528 he purchased for himself and his heirs a house in the quarter of the town called St. John's, for three hundred gulden. The official entry proves that he made the transaction personally.

Evidently Hans must have been profitably occupied in England, but, at the same time, the troubles that were later to overcloud the political horizon were looming near. Already King Henry, enamoured of Anne Boleyn, desired release from Queen Katharine, and the excitement consequent upon his efforts to obtain a divorce greatly affected public opinion. There had also been a scarcity in London, and the sweating sickness, as it was called, had snatched away many noble victims. The richer classes constantly changed from place to place to escape infection, and the king and Court seldom remained long in one spot. More's household had not escaped. The favourite daughter, "his darling Meg," was attacked, and was only saved from death by "a miraculous answer to her father's prayers." In addition to all this, a war between England and the country of Holbein's birth had occurred.

Holbein did not find Erasmus at Basel; probably he

stopped on his journey to deliver the picture to him at Freiburg, from which place Erasmus' letter of thanks was dated. Many causes had led to his departure from the city of his adoption. The dissensions between Church and State had gathered strength, and resulted in open riots and finally in hostilities. In the beginning of 1528 the Council had been forced to concede much to the popular demand; the Church service was simplified; the worship of Saints prohibited; pictures were removed from places of worship: but all concessions were in vain. The citizens, enraged and armed, insisted on the removal of the Catholic members of the Council, and went from one act of violence to another. The iconoclastic storm gathered and burst. On Shrove Tuesday the mob commenced their destructive work; they spared nothing that came within their reach, and during the whole of that and the succeeding day the work of demolition continued. Everything offensive to them that could be torn from the walls was burnt. No wonder Erasmus fled; he took up his sojourn in the neighbouring town of Freiburg, where Catholic opinions still retained their supremacy. We can imagine with what pain Holbein, though he sympathized with the enlightenment of the Reformation, must have regarded such brutal destructions.

Many of Holbein's earlier paintings no doubt perished in these outrages. His 'Last Supper' was torn and defaced, and his paintings for the organ-loft doubtless only escaped owing to the great height at which they were placed. He must have keenly felt the clause in the Order of Council passed in 1529, forbidding paintings in the churches, on the ground that they led to idolatry.

His first work on his return to Basel was a picture of his own family. We have no record of the condition in which he found them; one or two writers have endeavoured to draw a conclusion from the picture in question, that the wife and children were nearly starving during his absence, but certainly there is nothing in the painting itself to warrant this assumption. The picture is in the Basel Museum, and is a life-like representation of the group. Frau Elspeth holds in her embrace the little girl, whilst with one arm she draws the boy close to her. The wife has certainly not improved in her advancing years: coarse in feature and figure, there is a wide difference between her sorrow-stricken countenance here and the idealized Madonna of earlier years, or even the happy healthy girl's face in the Louvre sketch. The treatment of the picture is in strict keeping with Holbein's English portraits: there is the same clear flesh tint and strong bold outline. A copy of the original, most likely by the master's hand, is in the possession of Herr Brasseir at Cologne, but it is so defaced that no judgment on it is possible. The little boy standing by the mother's side appears about seven years of age, and is probably identical with the infant of the earlier sketches. He is a handsome child with a pathetic expression. The little girl is not more than two years of age. We have evidence that Holbein had other children, but they must have been born in later years. The son in the painting may be the same Philip Holbein who is more than once mentioned in letters written by the Basel Council. In 1548 he is spoken of as having finished his six years' apprenticeship, and as unable to obtain his release from his employer, Jacob David, a goldsmith in Paris; and again in a letter addressed to Philip himself, the Council tells him that they have taken measures for his return home. Further records inform us that Holbein left three daughters, who were all married, and whose names appear in Ludwig Iselin's account as having died between the years 1588 and 1612.

Thus we know with tolerable certainty that Hans Holbein's descendants were numerous, but we have no record that any of them were in any way remarkable.

At this time there was of course no painting to be done for religious purposes, and Holbein was probably obliged to content himself with designs for woodcuts and illustrations; but in 1530, the long interrupted painting for the "back wall" of the Town Hall was re-commenced and completed, for we have an entry respecting the payment of the sum given for it, and in it we find evidence of the painter's increased importance since his journey. Whilst before he left he received by instalments only seventy-two florins for the paintings in the Hall, we now find him paid more than half that sum for the narrow back wall alone.

None of his earlier compositions can compete with his 'Rehoboam,' of which an original drawing is in the Basel Museum. With excited gesture the young king is dismissing the Israelites, who are begging for a more merciful government. His raised finger emphasizes his words as he replies, "My Father has chastised you with rods, but I will chastise you with scorpions." A page, holding the scourge, gives meaning to the king's words. A glimpse into the future is given in the background where Jeroboam is being crowned by the revolted tribes. A smaller picture also evidently belongs to the Town Hall decorations: this is clear, in spite of much criticism to the contrary, because the same column appears in both pictures and one of the inscriptions in the Hall bore reference to it. It represents the meeting between Samuel and Saul. Saul has disobeyed the Lord in carrying away captive the Amalekite women and children. Samuel in anger comes to upbraid him, and is met by Saul with reverential gestures, while the captured people are in chains behind him. In the distance we see the burning villages and desolated country. But the prophet is not softened; and the painting conveys in the fullest manner the idea of his upbraiding words. Probably from the introduction of the flames and smoke in the sketch, Holbein intended some grand effect in chiaroscuro.

A third picture, also taken from the Old Testament history, completed the series, but we have no trace of it, save in the inscription, "Hezekiah compelling the breaking of the Idols." In this we can trace the spirit of the times which led to the iconoclastic storm.

After these paintings, our next notice of the artist is as receiving '17 Pfund 10 Shillings' for a most ordinary piece of work, a clock on the Rhine gate, which he probably had to decorate.

To the year 1530 belongs also a portrait of Erasmus, the original of which has the date inscribed on either side of the head. It is in the Parma Gallery, and was probably painted from the picture in Longford Castle; but the latter is much smaller, and the hands are differently placed. Three copies are extant, one in Vienna, another in Turin, and lastly one sent in 1532 from the Town Council of Basel to that of Rotterdam. Of the same period is probably also the celebrated woodcut of Erasmus, a large full-length portrait, inscribed, 'Erasmus Roterodamus im Gehäuse.' A copy of this portrait with a Latin verse complimentary to Erasmus was published by Froben's son in 1540 as a title-page to the collected works of Erasmus. An earlier edition appeared also, but it is uncertain at what date: in it the inscription is longer, consisting of two verses. There is no doubt that we are right in ascribing the portrait to the period after Holbein's first visit to England, because it coincides in every particular with his work at this time, both in the outline of the face, as well as in the designs of the surrounding frame, which are all of a renaissance character.

In these sad years at Basel, it must have been terribly hard to gain a living. A scarcity prevailed for two years, and the little river Birsig twice overflowed its banks and caused great damage. The wolves actually came into the town in the winter of 1529-30, a thing which never afterwards occurred. The excited religious feelings of the people led to terrible scenes of violence, and the differences of opinion between the Cantons ended in an open war.

Holbein's longing to return to England must have been great, and in 1531 we find traces of his presence in London in the portraits of two German merchants of the Steelyard. We therefore conclude that he must have commenced his second journey to England soon after the terrible winter of 1529-30. In the year 1532 he received an invitation from the Town Council to return to his home; they then held out as an inducement a promise of an annual pension of thirty pieces of silver for the support of his family; but the painter disregarded the summons, and in spite of the great changes which had happened in England, remained to try his fortunes once more. His old friend Sir Thomas More was no longer Lord Chancellor—the king in 1532, after much persuasion, had accepted his resignation—and was therefore unable to extend to the painter the same patronage as before: he had never amassed money during his stay in office, and now, in his altered circumstances, was possessed of a very modest income. Another patron of Holbein, Warham, Archbishop of Canterbury, died in this same year, protesting with his latest breath against the proposed Act of Parliament in favour of Henry's divorce.

Nevertheless, Holbein was now sufficiently well-known to be sure of constant occupation. We find him, immediately after his return to London, employed by his fellow-countrymen, the German merchants of the Steelyard in Thames Street. In the next few years his home was amongst them, and he enjoyed all the privileges of the members of the Hanseatic League. In the four years succeeding his return, we find many portraits of these German merchants, all having certain details in common. The most valuable of them is that of Jörg Gyze in the Museum at Berlin. Gyze belonged to an old Basel family: young, with long fair hair, but beardless, he wears a black coat with red under garments, so cut out at the top that the shirt with its fine pleating is seen on his bosom. He is seated at a table in a rich merchant's office, surrounded by every accessory that he could require; and before him is a glass of flowers, charmingly painted. A letter which he is about to open has the following address: "*Der erszamen Jergen Gisze to lunden in engelant mynem broder to handen*" (to the honourable Jörg Gyze in London in England my brother to his hands). This picture of Jörg Gyze is more particularly valuable as illustrative of Holbein's manner of treating his subject in the midst of every-day life. There is nothing in the least fanciful about it, and yet it is in the highest degree artistic.

Mr. Ruskin has given such a vivid description[1] of this portrait that we do not hesitate to transcribe it.

"In the portrait of the Hausmann George Gyzen, every

---

[1] "Cornhill Magazine," March, 1860.

HENRY VIII.

From the painting by Holbein, in the possession of the Earl of Warwick.

accessory is perfect with a fine perfection: the carnations in the glass vase by his side—the ball of gold, chased with blue enamel, suspended on the wall—the books, the steel-yard, the papers on the table, the seal-ring, with its quartered bearings,—all intensely there, and there in beauty of which no one could have dreamed that even flowers or gold were capable, far less parchment or steel.

"But every change of shade is felt, every rich and rubied line of petal followed: every subdued gleam in the soft blue of the enamel, and bending of the gold, touched with a hand whose patience of regard creates rather than paints.

"The jewel itself was not so precious as the rays of enduring light which form it, and flash from it beneath that errorless hand. The man himself,—what he was—not more; but to all conceivable proof of sight—in all aspect of life or thought,—not less. He sits alone in his accustomed room, his common work laid out before him; he is conscious of no presence, assumes no dignity, bears no sudden or superficial look of care or interest, lives only as he lived, but for ever . . . . Every detail of it wins, retains, rewards the attention with a continually increasing sense of wonderfulness. It is also wholly true. So far as it reaches, it contains the absolute facts of colour, form, and character, rendered with an unaccusable faithfulness. There is no question respecting things which it is best worth while to know, or things which it is unnecessary to state, or which might be overlooked with advantage.

"What of this man and his house were visible to Holbein are visible to us; we may despise if we will; deny or doubt we shall not; if we care to know anything concerning them, great or small, so much as may by the eye be known is for ever knowable, reliable, indisputable.

"Holbein is *complete* in intellect; what he sees, he sees with his whole soul; what he paints, he paints with his whole might. . . . . A grave man, knowing what steps of men keep truest time to the chaunting of Death. Having grave friends also;—the same singing heard far off, it seems to me, or, perhaps, even low in the room, by that family of Sir Thomas More; or mingling with the hum of bees in the meadows outside the towered wall of Basle; or making the words of the book more tuneable, which meditative Erasmus looks upon. Nay, that same soft Death-music is on the lips, even of Holbein's 'Madonna.'"

A portrait in Windsor Castle bearing the date 1532 is that of the goldsmith Mr. John of Antwerp,[1] as the address of a letter in his hands informs us. He was afterwards one of the executors of Holbein's will. A few years later he was the Court goldsmith, married an Englishwoman, and was recommended to the London Company of Goldsmiths by Thomas Cromwell as a candidate for membership. From the Basel sketches we find that Holbein had once designed a splendid drinking cup for him. As an indication of his calling, he is represented with a leather apron beneath his overcoat and with gold pieces lying before him. Another goldsmith of the same Company is known to us through an engraving by Wenzel Hollar. He is a thin man, homely in expression, but we can find no trace of the original which was in the Arundel collection; the engraving gives him as a half-length figure. A portrait of a young man with a thin and wonderfully

---

[1] Hans von Antwerpen.

attractive face, dark eyes and chestnut hair, wearing a black cap and black silk robe, is also in the Windsor collection: he is taken smaller than life-size, and we read his name upon the ground, Derick Born, aged twenty-three, and underneath a remark to this effect: "Give him but a voice and thou wouldst believe that he was living, not painted." A second portrait of him in the Munich Pinakothek gives only the head; it has been retouched, but is still valuable; it is painted on paper in oil.

According to a date inscribed on the back, a small round portrait of a man with brown beard, red waistcoat and black hat, now at Hanover, must be considered of this time. A portrait in the gallery of Herr Gsell, Vienna, belongs to the following year. The young man holds in his hand a pink, a flower which constantly appears in works of this date, and which probably had some political significance. The groundwork of this picture is blue and the colouring unusually bright.

To the year 1533 we must ascribe two half-length portraits of Merchants of the Steelyard, both very similar in detail; one, in the Brunswick Gallery, represents a man dressed in black, holding in his hand his gloves and a letter addressed "In London at the Steelyard." This picture also bears the motto "*In als gedoltig*" (Patient in all). The other, in the Belvidere at Vienna, has suffered some change in colour. The blue ground has become green, the grey shadows somewhat obscure the artistic power. The subject of this picture, also a young man, is opening a letter, which gives his name Geryck Tybis of Duisburg. A curious account of himself is given in the young man's own writing in another letter, lying by his side, thus: "When thirty-three years of age, I, Geryck Tybis of

London, looked like this, and I have marked in my own hand this portrait with my device, in the middle of March, 1533, by me GERYCK" (here the device is given). To the same group of Merchants, although it was painted a few years later, belongs a portrait of Derick Berck in Lord Leconsfield's collection at Petworth.

A large allegorical picture, representing the 'Wheel of Fortune,' now in the possession of the Duke of Devonshire, belongs to the year 1533; it is executed in body colours and contains four figures, the first climbing the wheel, the second sitting on the top of it, a third falling from it, and a fourth on the ground. The date and Hans Holbein's monogram are given, as well as several German inscriptions. The subject, which was familiar in Germany and Switzerland, makes it probable that it was painted for a countryman of the artist. This picture was shown at the Exhibition of Works by the Old Masters at the Royal Academy in 1873: the catalogue gives a very full description of it.

The year 1533 is remarkable in English history as that in which Henry VIII. obtained his long-desired divorce. He had married Anne Boleyn secretly about the 25th of January, and four months afterwards ordered brilliant preparations for her coronation. On the 19th of May Anne was conducted in great splendour from Greenwich to London, to spend the day before her coronation at the Tower. The king met her on the river with a vast number of barges, and when on the 31st she was brought from the Tower to Westminster to receive the crown in the Abbey Church next day, a pageant, more gorgeous than any that preceded it, was arranged. The streets of London were hung with flags and banners, and the various companies and guilds outvied each other in loyal demonstration. The Steelyard merchants were not behindhand, and their decorative designs were devised and arranged by Holbein. The chronicles of the day do not describe his production, but a drawing in the collection of Herr Weigel in Leipsic supplies us with a rough sketch of it in Indian ink, which is very characteristic of Holbein's manner. The architectural base is in the richest renaissance style; from it arises a triumphal arch, and on either side brackets support the stage. High above, sits Apollo crowned by the German Eagle and extending his hand as if in blessing; lower down are the Muses singing or making music on drums and pipes. A stone fountain at Apollo's feet is beautifully executed: at the corners are royal crowns surmounting coats of arms.

But the merchants of the Steelyard employed their countryman for higher designs than for merely passing shows. Two large pictures which decorated their guildhall were his work: one was the 'Triumph of Riches,' the other represented the 'Triumph of Poverty.' They were famous in their own day, and the writers of the sixteenth century mention several copies of them by Italian artists. Unhappily all trace of these paintings is lost to us. The Steelyard merchants had many reverses in later years: Queen Elizabeth took possession of their Hall and sent the Germans back to their own country, and when in King James's time the Hall was restored to them, everything was found mutilated or destroyed. The few paintings were presented by the League to Henry Prince of Wales. Their gift is mentioned by the Housekeeper Holtsho in January, 1616, with the comment that even if the paintings are old they might still be acceptable to Prince Henry.

Most likely they were in King Charles's splendid collection, but we meet with no notice of them after 1627, when Sandrart saw them in the Earl of Arundel's country house. Fortunately the original sketch of the 'Triumph of Riches,' which is preserved in the Louvre, gives us some idea of its beauty. It is a spirited design, drawn with a pen and shaded with Indian ink. In the British Museum there are fragments of a beautiful engraving of the year 1561, made probably from this sketch, bearing the date of Antwerp. Two copies of the painting, made by the Dutch artist Jan de Bischop, who died in 1686, are also in the British Museum. They are sketched with a pen and shaded in bistre; copies made by Zucchero in 1574 were in the last century in the collection of the Hesse-Darmstadt Privy Councillor Fleischmann at Strasburg; they were engraved in Chrétien de Mechel's Life of Holbein, and were doubtless the very copies which Sandrart says that he himself possessed.

The conception of the 'Triumph of Riches' is in accordance with the ideas of the day. Latin inscriptions and mottos are lavishly introduced into it. Plutus, the God of Wealth, represented as a bald-headed old man with a long beard, is sitting in an elegant golden chariot, bending forward as if overburdened by cares; sacks of gold are under his feet and a vessel full of money is before him. Below him sits Fortuna, a young and graceful woman, her eyes bound and her hair streaming in the wind; she scatters money amid the crowd of people that surround her: many of these are known as rich men, and the names of most are given. The entire representation is of course allegorical.

According to Van Mander, the 'Triumph of Poverty' bears a Latin motto in verse, the burden of which is, that

PORTRAIT OF AN ENGLISHMAN.

From a drawing in body-colour by Holbein, at Berlin.

he who is poor has nothing to fear: he is filled with joyous hope, for he hopes to acquire riches and learns by virtue to serve God. Poverty, a half-starved old woman, is represented in a wheelbarrow with Misfortune for her only companion: around her half-naked and starving figures, representing Mendicity, are threatened by her with a rod. Instead of fiery steeds, two donkeys, Stupidity and Inactivity, and two oxen, Negligence and Sloth, draw her vehicle along; but four beaming figures—Moderation, Industry, Activity, and Work—guide them. Hope holds the reins, and Diligence, Memory, and Experience are seated behind and distribute implements of labour to the poor, who surround them. Thus is self-help suggested. Dr. Waagen, in criticizing these paintings, says that they stand midway between Mantegna and Raphael.

Holbein's historical compositions at this time appear to have been very rare, but the Queen's collection at Windsor contains a drawing which bears strong internal evidence of being by him. It represents the 'Queen of Sheba before Solomon;' it bears no date, but it corresponds in treatment to the period of the Steelyard paintings. King Solomon sits enthroned in a grand building in the renaissance style, and receives the kneeling Queen of Sheba: noble women in pairs are behind her, and servants laden with costly presents kneel before the king. Latin versions of the queen's address, taken from 1 Kings x. 6-9, are inscribed in various parts of the picture. From Wenzel Hollar's engraving we gain but a poor idea of the beauty of the original drawing:[1] it is executed in metallic pencil with the usual

---

[1] A photograph of this drawing is included in "Specimens of Ten Masters," by B. B. Woodward, formerly the Queen's librarian.

Indian ink shading; here and there the drapery and points in the background are touched up with gold; fruits, green and red, are held up in a basket by one of the serving girls. The ground is blue with golden stars, and it is almost impossible to convey an idea of the admirable outlines of all the figures.

Two portraits, which hung side by side in the picture gallery of Count Schönborn in Vienna, must here be mentioned; of these the more beautiful is now in the Berlin Museum. It represents a half-length figure of a young man dressed in black against a blue background. An inscription, signed on the ground in gold, gives the date 'Anno 1533. Ætatis suæ 34.'

One of the most celebrated of Holbein's productions is a large painting belonging to the same year; it is a panel at Longford Castle, representing two life-size male figures. Upon the marble floor the painter has written 'JOHANNES HOLBAIN PINGEBAT 1533.' The name given for this painting, 'The Ambassadors,' seems less suitable than the later one, 'The Scholars,' for the entire surroundings of the figures bear reference to science and art. Both men are standing against a table with a double shelf. The principal figure of the two, a knightly personage in the prime of life, has slightly dark hair and the full short beard of the then prevailing fashion; his costume consists of a black garment with puffed sleeves, a brilliant red jerkin with green scarf and broad shoes; his golden necklace bears as a pendant a medal of St. Michael; a little hat placed somewhat awry is on the head. On the hilt of a dagger which hangs at his side is written 'ÆT. SUÆ 29.' He is looking straight at the spectator. The other figure stands a little further back and is dressed like a scholar of the day, in a doctor's hat and long brown silken robe with green stripes, fur lining and collar; his hair also is dark, and he wears a short beard. Close by his hand is a book with '*ætatis suæ* 25,' written on the edge of the leaves. The background is formed by a green curtain, the table and chairs are covered with astronomical and scientific instruments. A celestial and terrestrial globe are introduced, and the latter in particular is so nicely executed that the Latin names upon it may be easily read. A chant book, lying open, has a German Church song which may be plainly deciphered. The colouring of this renowned painting is very fine. Tradition gives the name of Sir Thomas Wyat to the courtier in this picture, and possibly this may be right, for we know that Wyat translated many of the German Church hymns. He was a man of great learning and versatility, and a particular favourite of Anne Boleyn. A likeness of the same personage in the Windsor drawings bears sufficient resemblance to the picture to support this view.

Sir Thomas Wyat died in 1541, and his biographer, John Leland, honoured his memory by a little book, which appeared in the following year, entitled "Nænia on the death of the Incomparable Knight Thomas Wyat." On the back of the title-page is a woodcut of a small circular profile of Wyat in Holbein's happiest manner; even the inferiority of the cutting cannot spoil the spirited effect. Perhaps we are right in imagining his companion in the painting to be the same John Leland, but we have no trustworthy corroboration of this surmise.

To the year 1533 belongs the portrait of Robert Cheseman, Royal Falconer; it is now at the Hague, and is said to be very fine. He is holding a falcon on his wrist, and his name, the date, and his age—forty-eight years—are written on the greenish-blue background.

In the Ambraser Gallery at Vienna are two little round pictures belonging to the following year, 1534: they represent a gentleman of a melancholy expression and a lady in a fur-trimmed dress, aged twenty-eight. The gentleman has on either side of him the letter H and R in gold embroidery. Both pictures are well preserved.

A portrait which we must next mention has a keen interest for all English readers: it is that of Thomas Cromwell. A sketch of his head in Wilton House is drawn with a light touch of colour upon a red tinted paper. A painting, also giving only the head, is in the possession of Captain Ridgway: in this work Cromwell wears a black cap, which entirely conceals the hair, and in both pictures we are reminded of the character of the man, who, a son of the people, battled through difficulties until he raised himself above the highest nobles. A larger painting in the possession of the Countess of Caledon, which was shown at the National Portrait Exhibition, must have been painted in 1534: it has been multiplied by Hollar's rare and beautiful engraving. Seated on a wooden seat, he holds a paper in his hand: pens, ink, a richly bound book and various documents are around him. One of the papers bears an address describing the person represented as the "Maister of our Jewelhowse," which sufficiently proclaims the date, as Cromwell was appointed Master of the Jewel Office in 1531, and was advanced to be First Secretary of State and Master of the Rolls in 1534.

Among the Windsor drawings we find a friend of Sir Thomas Wyat, John Poyns of Essex, who died in 1558, and another of Nicholas Poyns, who belonged to the elder branch of the same family. A son of his is also in the same collection, and in the background of that drawing the date and a French motto are still legible.

"JE OBAIS A QVI JE DOIS
JE SERS A QVI ME PLAIST
ET SUIS A QVI ME MERITE."

Two other portraits of gentlemen, not dated, probably belong to this epoch. At Frankfort-on-the-Maine there is a half-length picture of a young man in profile with a hat and feathers, holding a pink in his hand, who appears again in the Windsor collection as 'Simon George of Cornwall.' A portrait of another young man of the same county is in Hampton Court, and the original sketch is among the Windsor drawings: it is designated as 'Reskemeer, a Cornish Gentleman,' and is probably identical with a John Reskymer who was sheriff of the county in 1535.

A French poet, Nicholas Bourbon, who appeared in England at this time and who is also in the Windsor collection, became a great friend of Holbein. He is drawn in profile, and looks reflective and intelligent; he has long hair and a small beard, and somewhat recalls the features of Erasmus. Holbein adorned the later edition of Bourbon's poems with a woodcut of the author, and the poet in return wrote a laudatory introduction to the pictures from the Old Testament, which were now occupying Holbein's attention. A passage in one of Bourbon's verses speaks of Holbein as a miniature painter: his delicacy of treatment would have rendered it easy for him to attain this highest branch of his art, but we are unfortunately without sufficient data to enable us to distinguish the genuine works of the master from the numbers that are attributed to him. Of those which we really accept as his, that of little Henry Brandon, son of the Duke of Suffolk, is perhaps the most beautiful. A miniature of a younger brother, Charles Brandon, of later date, may also be seen at Windsor. It is singular that Holbein should have left no picture of the duke their father, as he was the companion of Henry VIII. and husband of the king's sister Mary. We have, however, a portrait of the mother of the two boys, Catherine, fourth wife of the duke. Another miniature in the Windsor library is undoubtedly the work of Holbein: it represents Elizabeth Lady Audley, the daughter of Sir Bryan Tuke, already painted by him. Her portrait appears on a larger scale among the Windsor drawings, and both works show the same jewels.

In 1535 we find Holbein giving full vent to his Protestant predilection, in his illustrations to the first complete English edition of the Bible. It was this book, splendidly finished, and now an extremely rare volume, which was published by Christopher Froschover at Zurich. The title-page was designed by Holbein, and the king appears amid a group at the base. Another title-page was his work, but only one copy of it exists—in the Royal Cabinet of Engravings in Munich.

In the same year he issued a small series of satirical woodcuts representing the Passion scenes. The book which originally contained the drawings has entirely disappeared, and our knowledge of it is entirely dependent upon Wenzel Hollar's engravings of sixteen of the series. It was in this year that Thomas Cromwell, now vice-regent for the king, appointed a general investigation of the monasteries. All the woodcuts bear a satirical reference to the time. The clergy in their rich possessions, with their miserly appropriations and utter disregard of the claims of the people; the monks, leaving their monasteries in quest of sinful and debauched pleasures; and various other scandals of the day are alluded to in them. The first scene, representing the 'Agony in the Garden,' shows Judas, disguised as a monk, having stolen the purse, leading in two figures in ecclesiastical attire. The second shows the priestly rabble falling down before the majesty of Christ, as He says: "I am He whom ye seek." A verse appended to the third, in which Peter cuts off the High Priest's servant's ear has also an anti-papistical significance; and throughout every possible allusion is made to the corrupt spirit of the religious orders of the time.

The same satire animates the wood-cut illustrations of Cranmer's Catechism, which, translated from the Latin, did not appear till some years later. Three of these drawings—'Moses on Mount Sinai,' and two others which were designed for this work—are undoubtedly by Holbein. The first represents the Saviour entering the porch of a church, pointing out, with significant finger, the self-righteous Pharisee; the second shows Him casting out a devil from the possessed man, whilst the Pharisees are represented by figures of monks and priests, wearing cowls and mitres and generally very stout in figure. In spite of the bad engraving we catch the dramatic intention of the author of these spirited woodcuts. Even less well engraved is a small illustration to an English Reformation pamphlet upon the words: "I am the good Shepherd: the good shepherd giveth his life for the sheep, but he that is an hireling fleeth," &c., where Christ is pointing out to

His disciples the faithless shepherd, who, in monk's attire, is running away as fast as he can, because the wolf attacks his flock. This little pamphlet and Cranmer's Catechism did not appear till five years after Holbein's death, but they were evidently designed at an earlier date and probably issued in private; for after Jane Seymour's death the Catholic party regained an ascendancy which would have prevented their circulation, and the publication had to be postponed until a new sovereign succeeded. Most of Holbein's designs were probably executed in the first instance in Switzerland, where the art of engraving had attained excellence earlier than in England.

A large folio woodcut, which appeared in Hall's famous Chronicle is undoubtedly from a design by Holbein. It represents Henry VIII. in council, in a rich apartment, the ceiling of which is highly decorated in the renaissance style. The king, with the full beard of the fashion after 1535, sits surrounded by his nobles and councillors, of whom there are twenty-seven differently engaged, some whispering, some listening, some reflecting. This representation of the monarch at this period leads us to imagine that Holbein entered the king's service earlier than has been supposed; but we cannot give any date with absolute accuracy. Our first positive information is from a letter from the poet Bourbon in 1536, in which Holbein is spoken of as the King's painter. A small half-length picture, supposed to be of Anne Boleyn, has been taken as confirmation of this, but the date, '1525, aged twenty-two,' proves the portrait to have been intended for some other Anne, possibly Queen Anne of Hungary.

Several other pictures of Anne Boleyn have been ascribed to Holbein, but we know of none that can be considered undoubtedly his. The portrait of the Duke of Richmond, Henry's natural son, who died in 1536, aged only seventeen, is attributed to Holbein: it was executed in 1534. But although we may infer from these doubtful cases that Holbein was in the king's service earlier, we can only begin an authenticated account of him as "his Majestie's servant" after Henry's marriage with Jane Seymour.

CHAPTER VI.

Death of Sir Thomas More—Death of Anne Boleyn—Marriage of Henry VIII. to Jane Seymour—The Windsor Drawings—Death of Jane Seymour—The Duchess of Milan—Holbein's Salary.

1534 TO 1537.

IT is scarcely possible that Holbein could have been indebted to his old patron, Sir Thomas More, for his introduction to King Henry and consequent appointment as Court painter, for the chancellor was at that time no longer in favour: probably Sir Thomas Wyat, who had great influeuce with the Court, obtained this favour for him.

In 1534 More expiated on the scaffold his opposition to the king's plea of the invalidity of his first marriage. This execution, which drew forth a universal cry of indignation, was two years afterwards followed by an event which was even more tragical. King Henry declared that his long-aroused suspicions of Anne Boleyn amounted to certainty, and upon the 19th of May, 1536, the unfortunate queen paid the penalty of her follies, if not of her sins, by death. On the following day the king married Jane Seymour, who at Whitsuntide was proclaimed queen. From this date we may look upon Holbein as in the king's service; evidently too in high favour, for we find him exonerated from many of the more menial offices which in those days fell to the lot of the Court painter. Henry employed several artists, among them Andrew Wright,

HENRY VIII. AND HIS FATHER HENRY VII.

who was house-decorator, so that Hans had more time to devote his energies to portrait painting; probably in other branches of his art he was oftener called upon to invent than to execute.

Before his entry into the service of the Court, Holbein had been extensively engaged in painting portraits. It would appear that this was from his own choice rather than from any want of subject; for from an inventory of the works of art which Henry VIII. possessed at Westminster, it is certain that the painters of the time had a wide range of subjects. But portraits were more highly esteemed and better paid for than other pictures. Holbein's portraits engrossed the whole powers of his mind. Nowhere is his skill more ably shown than in his first great masterpiece: it was a fresco painting, which unfortunately shared the fate of his earlier works at Basel. It was destroyed by fire in 1698; but happily Charles I. had ordered a copy to be taken of it, thirty years before, by a Flemish artist, and this copy, which is preserved in Hampton Court, has been engraved by Vertue. A precious fragment of the original cartoon is still jealously guarded by the Duke of Devonshire at Hardwick Hall; it is boldly traced with the brush in black-and-white distemper, evidently not with the idea of producing an effect, but solely for practical use in fresco-painting. From the engraving we learn that the picture contained life-sized figures of Henry VIII., his wife Jane Seymour, his father Henry VII., and his mother Elizabeth of York. The scene is laid in a stately hall; a carpet of beautiful device covers the floor. The two queens appear nobly arrayed, and Henry VII., tall, spare, and beardless, dignified yet simple in attire; Henry VIII., with his enormous bulk, standing in his favourite attitude with his legs apart, is attired in sumptuous magnificence; his manner of standing and of grasping his dagger seems to indicate the determined character of the man. This masterpiece is not only noticed by Van Mander, but is mentioned in the account of the Duke of Saxony's visit to England in 1613. It was the type which was successively followed in all King Henry's portraits, with most of which Holbein has been erroneously credited. We have never met with, either in England or abroad, any genuine oil-painting of Henry VIII. by Holbein; but Earl Spencer has a miniature which is undoubtedly by his hand. The king wears a grey jerkin and a brown overcoat, richly embroidered in gold; the whole is beautifully executed, and Henry's position, turning to one side, shows Holbein's artistic conviction that his features were better seen in profile. Henry was of a different opinion, and in later years Holbein, like the king's other painters, had to depict him in full face. A miniature of Henry, with a companion one of Jane Seymour, belonged to the late Mr. H. Danby Seymour. Apparently Holbein did not paint the king very often: doubtless the constant demand for the royal portrait was satisfied by inferior artists, who copied Holbein's originals.

In the Belvidere in Vienna there is a beautiful half-length painting of Jane Seymour, richly dressed; the fairness of her complexion, for which she was remarkable, is heightened by the cold grey tints and delicate shadows introduced. Wherever it was admissible the artist has added ornaments: the hands, lightly resting together, emerge from exquisitely finished cuffs of Spanish lace-work; the cap with its angular shape is very becoming, and in the fair face we read the evidence of the character which won Henry's esteem and made the queen so much beloved and regretted by the people.

Among the Windsor drawings are many female portraits taken by Holbein when he was Court painter: we have Lady Lister, Lady Hobbie, Lady Parker, and others, all more or less celebrated. The portraits of the Marchioness of Dorset, daughter of the Duke of Suffolk, and of Mary, Dowager Queen of France, deserve particular mention. Many of the sketches are adorned with jewels, which were plentifully worn at this period of English history. Superfluity of ornament is not always conducive to good effect, yet we cannot but admire a miniature in the possession of Count Casimir Lanckoronski, in Vienna, representing a young lady of about seventeen years of age, not exactly beautiful, but very pleasant-looking; she is richly dressed in black with slashings of red. This painting rivals the portrait of Queen Jane Seymour in execution.

The portrait of Lady Vaux at Hampton Court is similar in treatment, but a more simple toilet would have been better suited to this personage with her broad face: she holds a pink in one hand. Lady Elizabeth Vaux was five years older than her husband Lord Vaux, a fact which is sufficiently indicated by the drawings in the Windsor collection.

The Belvidere at Vienna contains a very life-like half-length portrait of a citizen's wife; her appearance is full of dignity and repose. A picture of a lady of middle age, holding a rosary in both hands, and a corresponding half-length picture of a man in black with a gloomy expression, are in the Cassel Gallery. This gallery contains many pictures erroneously imputed to Holbein; but, on the other hand, one hanging there attributed to Dürer which represents a man in knightly attire, may justly be claimed for the Augsburg master. A copy of this portrait, which may also be by Holbein, is in Herr Culemann's possession.

None of Holbein's later paintings rank higher than that of Sir Richard Southwell, in the gallery of the Uffizi in Florence. It is dated the 10th of July, in the twenty-eighth year of the reign of King Henry, and the age of the sitter is given as thirty-three. A splendid study for this painting is in the Windsor collection, and bears a note in Holbein's writing: "*Die Augen ein wenig gelbett*" (the eyes a little brownish). In the picture he wears a black cap with a jewel set in gold, a violet velvet coat, with black sleeves, and a gold chain. His character is well known from history: he treated with equal treachery both Sir Thomas More and the Earl of Surrey.

A portrait of Richard Rich, a citizen's son who rose to high office under Cromwell, and was made Lord Chancellor in the reign of Edward VI., is also in the Windsor collection. On another sheet is a far more beautiful and characteristic portrait of his wife Elizabeth, a noble-looking woman; from this sketch Holbein painted a half-length portrait, in the possession of Mr. Walter Moseley, of Buildwas Park in Shropshire, which has been erroneously exhibited as 'Katharine of Aragon.'

The portrait of Sir Edward Seymour, brother of the queen, subsequently Duke of Somerset and Protector of England, is to be found at Sion House, the residence of the Duke of Northumberland. Seymour is represented as a young man with a long pointed beard, darkly dressed, and wearing a hat and feathers: a medal suspended from a blue ribbon round his neck bears a St. George. Sir John Russel, who had been at Court since the reign of

Henry VII., and subsequently became Keeper of the Great Seal and first Earl of Bedford, is also in the Windsor collection. He is almost in profile, and from the inscription we learn that he was blind of one eye: his whole appearance is dignified and important. A finished picture from this sketch is in the possession of the Bedford family.

The Windsor collection contains also William Fitz-William, the Lord High Admiral in 1537; Edward Stanley, Earl of Derby (died 1574); Sir Thomas Strange (died 1545); Sir Thomas Wentworth (died 1551); and Charles Wingfield, of Kimbolton Castle, Huntingdonshire, a powerful man depicted with his hairy chest uncovered. There are also fair young Edward Clinton, subsequently Earl of Lincoln, who did not appear in public life until after Holbein's death; Thomas Parrie (died 1559), one of the few men who remained faithful to Elizabeth during her seclusion; Philip Hobbie, Groom of the King's Privy Chamber (died 1558), and William Sherington, Groom of the Robes. Hobbie we afterwards find mentioned as Holbein's travelling companion.

Of Sir Nicholas Carew, the king's Master of the Horse, there is a beautiful portrait in the possession of the Duke of Buccleuch. For many years Henry's friend and companion, he provided most skilfully for his amusement, and had great influence over him; but after the conspiracy of the Marquis of Exeter and Cardinal Pole, Henry became suspicious of him, and sent him to prison. He was beheaded in 1539.

We may close our list of portraits of this period by mentioning one which is deservedly celebrated—the splendid portrait of Morett in the Dresden Gallery. A mention of him in the Privy Purse expenses of Henry VIII. refers to him as "Hubert Morett, Jeweller;" his trade is also sufficiently indicated by a badge. Dressed in a jerkin and upper garment of black satin, he stands before us, overflowing with self-importance and wealth; in his hand he holds a magnificent dagger, probably of his own workmanship. This picture went through strange adventures: it was at one time in the gallery of the Duke of Modena, and when in 1745 the duke's collection was sold to the King of Saxony, the name of the picture was altered; it was then erroneously declared to be the portrait of 'Lodovico Sforza il Moro', by Lionardo da Vinci, and was thus catalogued until quite lately, when Hollar's engraving from the original drawing was hung side by side with the picture, and the error was speedily rectified.

A glimpse into the Court life of the time is given us in a small drawing shaded with Indian ink, which is in the British Museum. Henry VIII. sits at table alone under a canopy; the apartment is full of figures; servants bearing dishes are approaching him; the sideboard is completely covered with vessels; everything in miniature, yet everything perfect in execution, every detail clearly discernible. Two other sketches in pen and Indian ink, and both belonging to the same period, are in the Royal collection at Windsor: one represents a group of musicians, and the other is evidently intended for a family picture. In it a mother is bending over a child, which lies upon her lap on a pillow; other children are standing around her.

Holbein's designs for ornament deserve special mention. The drawing for the "Jane Seymour Cup," in the Bodleian Library at Oxford, is perhaps the most beautiful example of this class of art in the world. It is in the purest style of the renaissance, and is very valuable for

HUBERT MORETT, THE GOLDSMITH.

From the painting by Holbein, in the Dresden Gallery.

the information it gives us as to the style of decoration used at that period. Somewhat like in feeling to the works of Benvenuto Cellini, it is more refined, and we know of no work by the Florentine artist to equal this charming drawing. It was undoubtedly executed for Henry VIII. about the year 1537, as a present for Jane Seymour, whose motto, "BOUND TO OBEY AND SERVE," it twice bears. The intertwined initials "H I" are repeated several times amid a profusion of jewels. In the British Museum there is a sketch of this very drawing.

That this design was carried out in a real cup we have, fortunately, the best possible evidence. In Rymer's "Fœdera," vol. xviii. p. 236, we find a warrant dated 1625, An. I. Car. I., for the delivery of certain crown jewels to the Duke of Buckingham, and among others is named:—

"*Item*, a faire standing Cupp of Goulde, garnished about the Cover with eleaven Dyamonds, and two pointed Dyamonds about the Cupp, seaventeene Table Dyamonds and one Pearl Pendent uppon the Cupp, with theis Words *bound to obey and serve*, and H and I knitt together, in the Topp of the Cover Queene Janes Armes houlden by twoe Boyes under a Crowne Imperiall,—Weighing threescore and five ounces and a halfe."

Unhappily, we can too well imagine the ultimate fate of this interesting work, which, had it been preserved to the present day, would undoubtedly have ranked first among the celebrated art treasures of England.

A design for a clock, which was formerly in the collection of Horace Walpole, and is now in the British Museum, bears this inscription: "*Strena facta pro Anthony Deny camerario Regis quod initio novi anni* 1545, *Regi dedit;*" i.e., "New Year's gift made for Anthony Denny, the King's

Chamberlain, which he gave to the King on New Year's Day, 1545." The two children who surmount this design are very Raphaelesque in treatment.

A very elaborate drawing of a chimney-piece in pen and ink washed with colour, which likewise belonged to Walpole, is now in the British Museum. It is in the richest style of the renaissance, and as it bears the royal arms, was probably designed for one of King Henry's palaces. The sketch of a battle-piece in the upper part of the design is full of vigorous spirit.

Both in the gallery at Basel and in the British Museum there are collections of designs by Holbein which show the singular versatility of his genius—drawings of highly decorated dagger-hilts, sheaths, and sword-belts, jewelled ornaments, chains, lockets, and bracelets, book-bindings, coins, and medals, chased work, monograms, and heraldic seals, all drawn in the purest spirit of the *cinque-cento*, and all of the greatest use to the art workman of the present day. Many designs of the same character of which the original drawings are lost are happily preserved in the engravings of Wenceslaus Hollar.

In all these varieties of work there is certainly sufficient to prove the activity of Holbein's life at Court. We have evidence that the king valued him, and proved his confidence by sending him upon more than one mission of delicacy and importance: foremost amongst these was a journey to Brussels. Henry's wedded happiness with Jane Seymour was, unfortunately, but of short duration. When, in 1537, an heir to the throne was born, the king and the nation were alike filled with exuberant joy; but even before the rejoicings for the auspicious birth were at an end, most unhappily the queen died—history says from want of proper care and attention. This sad event cast a gloom over the whole kingdom, and Henry retired into complete seclusion. He remained at Westminster many months, until the Council persistently urged him to enter into some other matrimonial engagement. Many were the proposed candidates for the honour of Henry's alliance, and amongst them all none appeared more eligible than the young Duchess of Milan, who was herself a widow. Niece of the Emperor of Germany and daughter of the King of Denmark, she had been married, while still quite a child, to the Duke of Milan, who died less than a year after their union. The Emperor of Germany, who at this period was, for political reasons, desirous of Henry's alliance, hailed the idea with warmth, and a painter was forthwith in request to take the young lady's portrait. King Henry selected for this honourable enterprise his Court artist Holbein, and a letter from the ambassador John Hutton, dated from Brussels, to Cromwell, who was the main advocate of the alliance in England, gives us an account of the arrival in Brussels of the painter "Hans," and his companion Philip Hobbie, and of his interview with the young duchess. "The next day following," concludes the letter, "the said Lord Benedict came for Mr. Hans, who having but three hours space, hath showed himself master of that science; for it is very perffect, the other is but slobbered in comparison, as by the sight of both your Lordship shall perceive." From this we see both the rapidity of Holbein's painting, and also that a former picture had been painted; the result of this three hours' sketch is said to be the small panel now at Windsor, but some authorities state that the original painting is in Arundel Castle, in the Duchess of Norfolk's private apartments. The painter of the "slobbered picture" had represented the Duchess of Milan in full regal attire; Holbein, on the contrary, portrayed her in her daily attire of deep mourning. Very artistic is the effect of the black satin gown, lined and trimmed with sable, and the little black cap, which entirely conceals the hair. The charm of this masterly delineation lies in the child-like face with the widow's dignity. Henry was so enamoured with this picture that it is said he immediately sent her a proposal of marriage, to which she replied, she would gladly have accepted him had she possessed two heads. This answer, however, is fictitious, for she evidently was not personally indisposed to accept the king's hand. Somewhat later, when political differences threatened to prevent the marriage, Wriothesley urged her to confide in him her personal inclination. She blushed deeply and said, "*My* inclination! What am I to say?" And she added, smiling, "You know I am the Emperor's poor servant, and must obey his will." But Charles V.'s friendly feelings to England underwent a change, and the marriage never took place. In the list of Henry VIII.'s collection of pictures at Whitehall there is mention of a full-length portrait of the Duchess of Milan.

Holbein's journey to Brussels with Philip Hobbie is mentioned in the book of His Majesty's household expenses thus:—"Paymente in March: *item* paid to Philip Hoby by the kinge commandment certifyed by my lord privy seale lettre for his cost aund expences sent in all possible diligence for the kinge affaires in the parties of beyonde the See xxiij £ vj s viij d."

Soon after Lady-day 1538 Holbein is mentioned for the first time in the household accounts as receiving his salary, the quarterly amount due to him at the expiration of three months was £7 10*s.*, a sufficiently liberal salary in consideration of the money value of the time. We find, indeed, that his salary was higher than that of all the other Court painters with one exception: thus two Italian painters, Antonio Toto and Bartolommeo Penni, received together £12 10*s.* for the quarter, while Lucas Hornebaud we find receiving 55*s.* 6*d.* monthly. A proof of the favour in which Holbein was held is to be found in sundry entries of payments made in advance; for instance, in Midsummer, 1538, we find the following: "*Item* for Hans Holbyn paynter for one hole yeres annutie aduanced to him before hand the same yere to be accompted de from our lady dey last past the somme of 30*l.*" Again at Michaelmas it stands: "*Item* for Hans Holbyn paynter wage—nihil quia solutum per warrant." Of course he had also nothing to receive at Christmas; still we find the following: "*Item* payde to Hans Holbyn one of the kinge's paynters by my lord pryvi seals lettre 10*l.* for his coste and charge at this tyme sent abowte certeyn his grace affares into the parties of High Burgony by way of his grace rewarde." We have no means of absolutely knowing the object of this mission, but it appears probable that the Duchess of Milan may at this time have been in Burgundy, and that Holbein's business was either to paint her portrait again, or to convey to her the portrait of her royal admirer. However this may be, Hans profited by the opportunity to go into Switzerland, for in December of the same year we hear of him at Basel. A letter of this date from Rudolph Gwalther, who was then studying at Basel, to an artist named Bullinger in Zürich, says: "Hans Holbein came hither recently from England on his way to Basel. You can scarcely imagine how he extols the affairs of that happy kingdom. After a few days he will return there again." Dr. Iselin in his record says: "When he returned to Basel from England he was attired in silk and velvet; before this he was obliged to buy wine at the tap." This short record is of interest, coming from a man who lived near enough to Holbein's time to have heard of him authentically; besides, it furnishes us with the only personal details of this time with which we are acquainted.

CHAPTER VII.

Visit to Basel—Death of Sigismund Holbein—Return to England—Portraits of the Prince Edward—Anne of Cleves—Duke of Norfolk—Lady Catherine Howard—Lady Catherine Parr—The Barber-Surgeons' Company—Death of Holbein—His last Will.

1538 TO 1543.

IN the year 1538 Holbein must have been at the very height of his fame. To Basel, the adopted town from which his poverty had driven him in his early days, he now returned in the character of a chosen envoy of the King of England, and upon a mission of the greatest delicacy. He had but just finished the portrait of the royal princess whom his sovereign was wooing, and his fame as a painter was on every tongue.

He had certainly shown no particular desire to return to Switzerland. The pension offered to him by the municipality of Basel had been too slight an inducement. Twice during his long absence his turn had come round for the military service of his guild. But now things were altered. He was in an official position at the Court of a foreign sovereign, receiving money for service to a foreign king, and this no citizen of Basel was permitted to do without express concession from the council. To obtain leave for further absence his presence there was a matter of necessity, and nothing could better demonstrate the estimation in which he was held by his fellow-citizens than a letter written by the Council of the city of Basel, dated the 16th day of October, 1538. The document is tolerably long, but we can give a concise abstract of its contents. The Council, first setting forth the reason for their offer, which they found in his extraordinary talents, proceeded to settle upon him a pension of fifty gulden yearly, provided he would return to his adopted city; and at the same time accorded him permission, in consideration of his having entered the service of the King of England, to remain in England two years longer, that he might receive an honourable discharge: and during that period his wife and children were to receive a sum of forty gulden a year. They also granted him leave to paint for other foreign kings, princes, and nobles, and two or three times yearly—though never without expressed permission—to travel to France, England, Milan, and the Netherlands, but only in an honourable and open manner.

We have no record of Elsbeth Holbein ever having received her pension, but she may have been paid out of the old monastery revenues, of which no mention would appear in the town accounts. The pension must, however, have lapsed, as Holbein did not return at the time specified, and meanwhile his family were assisted in another manner. In November, 1540, Sigismund Holbein died. In his will he states: "I bequeath to my dear Nephew Hans Holbeyn the painter. . . all my goods and property which I have and leave in the city of Berne;" and in January, 1541, the wife of "Meister Hansen" succeeded to the property after her son Franz Schmid, whom we have already mentioned, had been as her agent to Berne, to arrange for her proper receipt of the property. Thenceforth she must have been well provided for, without her husband's assistance.

Holbein was again in England at the beginning of the year 1539, for his New Year's gift to the king is mentioned: "By Hans Holbyn a table of the picture of the Prince's grace." The king's return present to the painter shows the esteem in which he held him. The royal gift was "a gilt cruse with cover," instead of the usual gift in money. The little Prince of Wales, whose portrait Holbein presented, must have been a handsome child, and Froude, in his History, tells how precious he was to his father; so much so, that no one except his personal attendants could obtain access to his rooms without a letter of admission. A beautiful portrait of him is in the Welfen Museum in Hanover, and a copy of it is in the possession of the Earl of Yarborough. An original study for the boy's head is in the Windsor collection. A few months later another larger portrait of the prince was taken; it is now in Sion House; the child's hands are without the rattle, which appears in the earlier portraits. A very pretty sketch of the same boy, playing with his dog, is in the Basel collection; from the style it would appear to have been intended for some plastic work.

Early in 1538 Henry's matrimonial intentions with regard to the Duchess of Milan were finally disappointed, and after the year which had been lost in this fruitless wooing, it was deemed expedient to arrange another marriage. Cromwell's Protestant predilections led him to regard the Duchess of Cleves as an eligible lady. Holbein was despatched to take her portrait, and hence arose the time-honoured legend that it was owing to his flattering representation that Henry decided to make her his queen. But this oft-repeated tale has no real foundation. This is clear, because Henry's advances were made before Hans set out on his journey. Two years earlier Hutton, the English Ambassador, in writing to Cromwell about the duchess, said: "The Duke of Cleves hath a daughter, but I here no great preas, neyther of her personage nor beawtie;" and the king himself, in his later complaints, speaks only of having been misled by what he had heard of her. However, all records agree in saying that she was amiable and beloved by the lower classes, while the more exacting ladies of the Court ridiculed her foreign manners. Holbein's picture of her in the Louvre is not unpleasing; her countenance is good and regular in feature, she has beautiful eyebrows, but her face is utterly devoid of expression. Of good height, she stands as if waiting a word of command, as though she had been painted full face without moving a muscle. Her grand Court dress is in almost painful contrast with her simple personal appearance. In addition to this painting there is also an original sketch from life at Arundel; and a miniature which was in the collection of Captain Meyrick at Goodrich Court. The poor queen was much to be pitied; although for a long time Henry's dislike was secret, and he appears never to have treated her otherwise than kindly.

In the midst of the splendid festivities which followed the celebration of the nuptials, Cromwell, the chief promoter, was raised to the rank of Earl of Essex. Holbein also was high in favour, and it is very likely that the German princess interested herself for her countryman, and certainly the wedding must have given plenty of occupation to all the artists attached to the Court. It is again recorded that the painter received payment in advance in September, and with an addition of £1 to his salary. Later, we find that he again received the same three

ANNE OF CLEVES.

From the painting by Holbein, in the Louvre.

quarters' money, which suggests the idea that the king gave him the surplus for some extra work, or as a mark of his approval. We never find entries of similar generosity in the household accounts to other painters, but it may possibly have been done to induce Holbein to disregard the summons home from the Council of Basel. In the later entries we find no further mention made of the increase of salary, but then Henry was once more involved in matrimonial difficulties. Shortly after midsummer the king ordered Anne of Cleves to retire to her palace at Richmond, and on the 12th of July she was divorced. Contemporary writers assert that she received the news of her downfall patiently and quietly. Her fall was preceded by that of her chief supporter, Cromwell, who had been arrested on the 10th of June. On the 28th of the next month he was beheaded.

Henry followed up this arbitrary act by condemning three Protestants to the stake, and already on the 8th of the following August he had found a new partner in Lady Catherine Howard, a rigid Roman Catholic: her influence can be easily traced in the rapid ascendency of the Papist party. Foremost amongst them was the Duke of Norfolk, whose portrait by Holbein, or rather a copy of it, may be found at Windsor; another is at Arundel Castle. The original is unfortunately lost, but the copy gives ample evidence of the masterly power bestowed upon it. The brownish tint of the flesh was natural to the duke, and his thin face is full of force and vigour. We know also, from an undoubted source, that Holbein painted a portrait of the Earl of Surrey, the son of the Duke of Norfolk; for in a large picture by Philip Fruytiers, after Van Dyck, painted just a century later, the Earl of Arundel is shown sitting with his family in a room surrounded by portraits by Holbein; and one of these is a likeness of the young Earl of Surrey, whose name is legibly inscribed on it. Two sketches of him from life are also in the Windsor collection.

Most likely Holbein painted the new queen, but no positive evidence of this fact is to be found, although a miniature representation of her in the Windsor Library is ascribed to him. It is impossible to tell whether it was owing to party influence that there are far fewer pictures of Holbein to be traced after the fall of Anne of Cleves; certainly the household accounts seem to show that he was treated with less liberality. Although the painter still received his salary in advance, it was no longer for such lengthened periods. Half a year's payment is recorded in advance at Michaelmas, 1540, and another at Easter in 1541, and he apparently no longer occupied the apartments which had been granted him at Whitehall, for in the Subsidy Rolls in the city of London of the 24th of October, 1541, the name of Hans Holbein occurs among the strangers in Aldgate Ward in "the Parishe of St. Andrewe Undershafte," where he had to pay £3 out of his salary of £30.

In October of the same year Henry ordered a thanksgiving service for the blessing of a virtuous wife, and the very next day Cranmer opened his eyes to some of the queen's suspicious intrigues. The Protestant party used every available means to inflame the king's anger, and on the 13th of February, 1542, Catherine Howard was beheaded. After a short interval the king married a widow, Lady Catherine Parr. There is no portrait of her which we can trace to Holbein, but he painted that of her brother Sir

William Parr. The original sketch for this picture is in the Windsor collection, where also we find William Brooke, Lord Cobham.

It may have been owing to some loss of Court favour that to this period belong two portraits of persons of less consequence. In the Vienna Belvidere there is a portrait of a young man, aged twenty-eight, who is evidently of the citizen class: it is dated 1541. Attired in a black fur overcoat and a violet jerkin, he is sitting by a table, holding his gloves in his hands, after a favourite fashion in Holbein's pictures. Another portrait, also of 1541, gives us a man of thirty-seven years of age; he also holds his gloves in his hand: it is now in the Berlin Museum. In the Städel Museum at Frankfort is a large chalk drawing of a young man of thoroughly English character.

To the year 1542 belongs a small portrait in the Gallery at the Hague, the finest of Holbein's productions to be found there. It represents a young man of twenty-eight years of age, with broad countenance and reddish beard. On his left hand a falcon is poised, whilst in the right hand he holds the hood.

One of Holbein's most perfect pictures is the life-size, half-length portrait of an unknown man, which now belongs to Mr. John Millais. It was exhibited at the Dresden Holbein Exhibition, and attracted universal attention. It represents a man of fifty-four years of age, with prominent nose, and a grey beard, which fully justifies Van Mander's enthusiastic accounts of Holbein's success in the representation of beards.

The Trustees of the National Gallery have lately purchased, at the sale of Mr. Anderdon's collection, a portrait of Martin Luther, by Holbein, which was probably painted about this period. This is the only work by the master in the national collection, and is on that account very valuablo.

The largest of all Holbein's pictures belongs to this year or the next: it is a representation of 'King Henry granting the Charter to the Wardens of the Barber-Surgeons' Company,' and is still to be seen in their large hall in Monkwell Street. A strange difference in the treatment of some of the figures has led to a suggestion that it was only partly painted by Holbein, and this idea is rather strengthened by the date. The Charter was not granted to the Barber-Surgeons till 1540 or 1541: therefore the picture could only have been begun after that date, and must in any case have taken some time to complete. The inference must be, that though the whole composition may have been designed by Holbein, he did not live to finish it. The figure of the king is unquestionably not his work: Henry is seated on a throne, which was probably the painter's original intention, but the inartistic position and details of the king's portrait are sufficient proof that it was not painted by the master himself. The features were probably copied from the Whitehall picture. Some of the heads of the other figures have been spoilt by an attempt to retouch them, and others again are the work of a very inferior hand.

Two of the Masters of the Barber-Surgeons' guild were painted by him, and they are easily to be recognized in the large picture. They were Sir William Butts and Dr. John Chambers, both Physicians in Ordinary to the King. The portrait of Sir William Butts has been very much disfigured by retouching. He died in 1545, and has been rendered immortal by Shakespeare's introduction of him in his play of "Henry VIII." The half-length pictures of Sir William

THE DUKE OF NORFOLK.

From the painting by Holbein, at Windsor Castle.

and Lady Butts, which were in the National Portrait Exhibition of 1866, are both in the possession of Mr. W. H. Pole Carew.

Holbein undoubtedly painted the portrait of Dr. John Chambers in the Vienna Belvidere: eighty years of age, as he is reported to have been, he appears a venerable old man with a serious expression of countenance. This picture may be considered one of those which placed Holbein at the head of his profession as portrait painter.

In 1543 Holbein again painted his own portrait—at the age of forty-five—as it appears in a miniature in the possession of the Duke of Buccleuch; perhaps this is not the original, though probably it may be a copy made at the same date. Vorsterman and Hollar engraved it, and it is mentioned by both Van Mander and Sandrart. The features in the miniature, in spite of the difference in age, bear a distinct resemblance to the youthful portrait in the Basel Museum. The same calm, thoughtful eye is found in both; the projecting chin of the early picture is covered in the latter by a crisp beard; he is dressed in black, and holds a pencil in his right hand. This is the last known of Holbein's works.

In 1543 occurred the most violent pestilence of King Henry's reign. The old chronicler Hall says: "Thys yeare was in London a great death of the pestilence, and therefore Mighelmas terme was adiourned to Saint Albones and there was it kept to the ende." In early life Holbein had more than once made acquaintance with the plague in Basel, and he, like others, must have dreaded its attacks. So sudden were the seizures of this fearful sickness that those who were stricken in the morning were dead at noonday. The infection spared neither age, condition, nor sex: and in the very midst of this pestilence it is now known that Hans Holbein died. For many years it had been a generally received opinion that Holbein died of the plague, and it is probable that such was the case, although, until lately, the date of his death had been placed in 1554. This error was corrected by the discovery (in 1861) of Holbein's Will in the archives of St. Paul's Cathedral. It is as follows:—

"*In the name of God the father, sonne, and holy gohooste,* I, JOHNN HOLBEINE, *servaunte of the Kynges Magestye, make this my Testamente and last will, to wyt, that all my goodes shalbe sold and also my horse, and I will that my debtes be payd, to wete, fyrst to Mr Anthony, the Kynges servaunte, of Grenwiche, ye summe of ten poundes thurtene shyllynges and sewyne pence sterlinge. And more over I will that he shalbe contented for all other thynges betwene hym and me. Item, I do owe unto Mr John of Anwarpe, goldsmythe, sexe poundes sterling, which I will also shalbe payd unto him with the fyrste. Item, I bequeythe for the kynping of my two Chylder wich be at nurse, for every monethe sewyne shyllynges and sex pence sterlynge. In wytnes I have signed and sealed this my testament the vij^th day of Octaber, in the yere of o^r Lorde God M^l vCxliij. Wytnes, Anthoney Snecher, armerer, Mr John of Anwarpe, goldsmythe before sayd, Olrycke Obynger, merchaunte and Harry Maynert, paynter.*"

The next two paragraphs are translations from the original Latin.

"*On the 29th of November in the aforesaid year of our Lord, John of Antwerp appointed executor in the Will or last Testament of John alias Hans Holbeine, recently deceased in the Parish of St Andrew Undershafte appeared before Master John Croke, Commissary General and resigned the execution of the Will, which renunciation was allowed and the administration of the property left was consigned to the before mentioned as sworn in and was admitted and accepted by him. The rights of each intact. Date,"* &c.

"*Holbene.*—— *The 29th of said month, the administration of the property of John alias Hans Holbene and recently deceased ab intestato in the Parish of St Andrew Undershafte was consigned to John of Antwerp as sworn in and was admitted and accepted by him, the right of each intact. Said day of month,"* &c.

Any further confirmation of Holbein's death about this time cannot be needed, but we have one in a letter (from which we have already quoted) from the Burgomaster Meyer of Basel to Jacob David, the goldsmith of Paris, the master of Philip Holbein, which, dated November 19, 1545, speaks of the father, Hans, as already dead.

Holbein was evidently supported in his last hours by his friend John of Antwerp, who alone appears as executor. He was a goldsmith of much repute, whose portrait Holbein had painted; the merchant Ulrich Obynger was probably from the Steelyard.

No mention whatever is made of Holbein's wife or family. But this omission is not, as has been supposed, owing to Elspeth's death, but more probably because the Will relates entirely to his English connections, and in no degree to the family in Basel, who, from all accounts, appear to have been well provided for.

The Basel archives contain an inventory of the effects of Frau Elspeth, dated the 8th of March, 1549, taken shortly after her death. From it we gain an insight into the prosperous condition of the family, enumerating, as it does, several beds, chests full of linen, various household appurtenances, and several silver vessels, similar to those described in Sigismund Holbein's will.

Thus, far from his country, but apparently honoured and prosperous, Hans Holbein was cut down in the prime of his manhood, and no records available to us have as yet thrown any light upon the more intimate relations of his life. His fame rests entirely upon those wonderful creations of his genius which have been preserved to us, and although future discoveries may increase our admiration of his character as a man, nothing that can be told of him can add to his eminence as an artist.

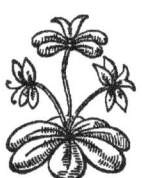

APPENDIX.

NOTE I.

Much confusion has arisen in the endeavours to fix with accuracy the year of Holbein's birth. The natural obstacles to obtaining trustworthy information at a distance of time were multiplied in Hans Holbein's case by an uncertainty which long existed as to the actual place of his birth. This doubt probably arose from his having obtained the freedom of the city of Basel in the year 1520, which led to the supposition that he was a native of that place.

Further and more serious complications arose, when in later times it was definitively settled that he was a native of Augsburg, upon the discovery that many of the documents and inscriptions relating to the supposed year of his birth were found to be forgeries. Foremost amongst these was an inscription in old Latin characters upon an altar-panel, now in the Augsburg Museum. The painting which represented the 'Death of St. Catherine,' was attributed to Hans Holbein the younger, as this name stands upon the frame, and on a votive tablet above the date 1512. When, in 1854, this panel was cleaned and restored, the reverse panel was separated from it, and an inscription came to light, written upon an open book, which in the picture lies upon St. Anna's lap. The translation is as follows:—

"By order of the worthy and most pious mother Veronica Welser, executed by Hans Holbein of Augsburg, at the age of seventeen."

This inscription was accepted by the highest German authorities as genuine, and upon its evidence Dr. Woltmann based his view that the birth of the world-renowned painter took place in 1495.

After the publication of the first edition of his biography, a later inspection of the inscription, which was rendered possible by the death of the custodian of the Augsburg Gallery in 1870, proved the entire inscription to be a modern forgery. Upon the application of turpentine the whole of the writing disappeared, and traces of a former inscription torn and defaced were found.

The discovery of the fictitious nature of this inscription led to further investigation, which resulted in a complete reversal of the then accepted date. Dr. Woltmann now gives it as his settled opinion that Hans Holbein the younger first saw the light in or about the year 1497.

A further confirmation of the fact that Hans Holbein, painter of Augsburg, was the father of the celebrated Hans Holbein, is found in a letter from the Burgomaster of Basel to the Vicar of Isenheim in Alsace, in which he claims for Hans Holbein the painting materials left him by the will of his father. This letter coincides with an entry in the Augsburg Register, that Hans Holbein, painter, left that city in order to execute a commission at Isenheim.

NOTE II.

This Table was referred to by Patin in the seventeenth century, but was neglected and forgotten until Professor Vögelin called attention to it in 1871, when it was placed in the Holbein Exhibition at Dresden.

It is engraved in "Die Graphischen Künste," edited by Dr. Oskar Berggruen (Vienna, 1880).

THE FOX-CHASE.

LIST OF HOLBEIN'S PAINTINGS AND DRAWINGS, CHRONOLOGICALLY ARRANGED.

A.D. 1515 TO 1520.

Two Portraits, a Man and Woman	Basel.
Painted Table at Zurich	Zurich.
"Praise of Folly." *Pen-and-ink drawings for* . .	Basel.
Schoolmaster's Signboard	Basel.
Portrait of Jacob Meyer	Berlin.
„ the wife of Jacob Meyer	Berlin.
„ Hans Herbster	E. Northbrook.
„ a Youth. *With Holbein's mark,* HH . .	Hermitage.
Adam and Eve. (*Half-length figures*) . .	Basel.
Virgin and Holy Child. *Lucerne, in the background* .	Basel.
Descent from the Cross. *Painted for a church* .	Basel.
Herstenstein House, Decorations of. *Copy of* . .	Lucerne.
The Last Supper. *Painted on wood*	Basel.
The Fountain of Life. *Signed,* IOHANNES HOLBEIN .	Lisbon.
Portrait of Jörg Schweiger	Basel.
Altar Panels, Two—Birth of Christ, Adoration of the Magi . . . . . . *In the Minster*	Freiburg
The Passion, Eight scenes of. (*In one frame*) . .	Basel.
„ Ten drawings of	Basel.
„ Seven drawings of. *In Indian ink* .	Brit. Mus.
Portrait of Bonifacius Amerbach	Basel.

1520 TO 1527.

A Dead Christ	Basel.
Christ the Man of Sorrows, and His Mother. *Diptych*	Basel.
Decoration for the Cathedral Tower	Basel.
St. Ursula, with the Arrow	Carlsruhe.
St. George, with the Dragon	Carlsruhe.
St. Elizabeth. *A Drawing*	Basel.
Madonna, with the Holy Child. *Drawn in imitation of a statue of wood*	Basel.
„ alone. *For glass painting*	Basel.
Two Mercenaries. *Drawn for glass painting*	Basel.
Costume Figures. *Five Drawings*	Basel.
The Son of the Unjust Judge. *A large drawing*	Dresden.
The Solothurn Madonna	Solothurn.
Drawing of the same subject . *In the possession of*	Herr Weigel.
The Meyer Madonna	Darmstadt.
Wall Decorations. *Drawings for*	Basel.
The Peasants' Dance. *A highly-coloured chalk drawing*	Basel.
Town Hall Decorations. *Original drawings of*	Basel.
Portrait of Froben	Hampton Ct.
„ Erasmus	Hampton Ct.
„ Erasmus. (*Earl of Radnor's*)	Longford Cast.
„ Erasmus. (*Formerly in King Charles's Coll.*)	Louvre.
„ Erasmus. *Three-quarter face, small circular*	Basel.
„ Erasmus	Turin.
„ Erasmus	Vienna.
„ Melancthon	Hanover.
„ Holbein. By himself. *Lightly-coloured*	Basel.
Coat of Arms for Waldenburg Rhine Gate	
Portrait of Lady, inscribed "Lais Corinthiaca"	
„ the Same—as Venus	Basel.

1527 AND 1528.

Portrait of Sir Thomas More	Mr. Huth.
„ Sir Henry Wyat. *Half-length*	Louvre.
„ Sir Thomas More. *Two drawings*	Windsor.
„ Warham, Archbishop of Canterbury	Lambeth Pal.
„ the Same. *Drawing*	Windsor.
„ John Fisher, Bishop of Rochester. *Drawing*	Brit. Mus.
„ John Fisher, Bishop of Rochester. *Drawing*	Windsor.

Portrait of Sir Henry Guildford (*Engraved by Hollar*)	Windsor.
" " " *Drawing* . . .	Windsor.
" Lady Guildford. (*Engraved by Hollar*) .	Mr. Frewen.
" a Man	Dresden Gall.
" Nicolas Kratzer	Louvre.
" Thomas Godsalve and Son. *Panels* . .	Dresden.
" Thomas Godsalve. *Of later date* . .	Windsor.
" Sir Bryan Tuke. *Signed*, I. O. HOLBEIN .	Munich.
" the Same. (*Known as the Ecclesiastic*) .	D. of Westm.
" Sir Thomas Elyot. *Drawing* . . .	Windsor.
" Lady Elyot. *Drawing*	Windsor.
" a Man of Middle Age	Madrid.
" a beardless Ecclesiastic	Pourtales Coll.

1528 TO 1531.

Sir Thomas More's Family. *The original picture is lost.*	
Original sketch of the Same, with notes	Basel.
Portraits of Holbein's Wife and Children . . .	Basel.
Original copy of the same	Brasseur Coll.
Designs for Dagger Sheaths	Berlin.
Town Hall. *Paintings for back wall of* . . .	Basel.
Original drawings for the same, Rehoboam, Samuel, and Saul	Basel.
Clock at the Rhine Gate. *Coloured.*	
Portrait of Erasmus	Parma.

1532 AND 1533.

Portrait of Jörg Gyze of the Steelyard	Berlin.
" John of Antwerp. (*In King Charles's Coll.*)	Windsor.
" a Young Man . (*Count Schönbrun's Coll.*)	Vienna.
" Hans von Zurich. (*Engraved by W. Hollar*)	
" a Man	Welfen Mus.
" a Young Man . . . . *Gsell Gallery*	Vienna.
" Derich Born	Windsor.
" a Merchant. *Ambrose Faller (?)* . .	Brunswck Gall.
" Geryck Tybis. *With letter bearing address*	Belvidere.
" Himself. (*In private possession*) . .	Vienna.
The Wheel of Fortune	Chatsworth.
Coronation Decorations. *Large drawing of* . .	Weigel Coll.
Triumph of Poverty. *Painting for the Steelyard* .	Lost.

Triumph of Riches. *Painting for the Steelyard*	Lost.
" " *Original sketch by Holbein*	Louvre.
" " *Engraving. (A fragment)*	Brit. Mus.
Queen of Sheba. *Drawing. (Engraved by Hollar)*	Windsor.
Portrait of a Young Man	Berlin Gal.
The Ambassadors, large painting, called. *Signed* IOHANNES HOLBEIN PINGEBAT 1533	Longford Cast.
Portrait of Robert Cheseman. *The Falconer*	The Hague.

1534 AND 1535.

Portrait of a Lady	Vienna.
" a Man. *Letters R. and H. introduced*	Vienna.
" Thomas Cromwell. *On tinted paper*	Wilton House.
" Thomas Cromwell	Capt. Ridgway.
" Thomas Cromwell	Lady Caledon.
" Anna Boleyn. *A Miniature*	Mr. S. Bale.
" Henry, Duke of Richmond	Mr. S. Bale.
" John Poyns, of Essex. *Drawing*	Windsor.

1535.

Portrait of Nicolas Poyns. *Drawing*	Windsor.
" his Son, Nicholas Poyns	Windsor.
" the Same. *Half-length* . *Private Coll.*	Paris.
" Simon George. *Half-length*	Frankfort.
" the Same. *Drawing*	Windsor.
" Reskymeer, a Cornish gentleman	Hamptn Court.
" the Same. *Drawing*	Windsor.
" Nicolas Bourbon. *Drawing*	Windsor.
" a Child, Henry Brandon. *Miniature*	Queen's Lib.
" the Duchess of Suffolk	Windsor.
" Lady Audley. *Miniature*	Windsor.
" the Same. *Drawing*	Windsor.

1536 AND 1537.

Portrait of Lady Richmond	Windsor.
" Henry VIII. and his Father. *Fragment of the original Cartoon*	D. of Devonsh.
" King Henry VIII.	Mr. Seymour.
" King Henry VIII. *Miniature*	Althorp Gal.
" King Henry VIII. *Miniature*	Mr. Seymour.
" Lady Vaux	Hampton Ct.

Portrait of Queen Jane Seymour. *Miniature* . .	Mr. Seymour.
„ the Same . . . . *Belvedere* .	Vienna.
„ the Same. *Drawing*	Windsor.
„ Lady Lister. *Drawing*	Windsor.
„ Lady Hobby. *Drawing* . .	Windsor.
„ Lady Parker. *Drawing* . .	Windsor.
„ Lady Meutas. *Drawing* . .	Windsor.
„ Lady Ratcliffe. *Drawing* . . .	Windsor.
„ Marchioness of Dorset. *Drawing* .	Windsor.
„ Lady Monteagle. *Drawing* . .	Windsor.
„ Lady Butts. *Drawing* . . .	Windsor.
„ Mrs. Souch. *Drawing* . . .	Windsor.
„ Lady Borow. *Drawing* . . .	Windsor.
„ Lady Vaux. *Drawing* . . .	Windsor.
„ Lord Vaux. *Drawing* . .	Windsor.
„ a Beardless Man . . .	Cassell Gall.
„ Sir Richard Southwell . . .	Uffizi Gallery.
„ the Same, with note by Holbein. *Drawing*	Windsor.
„ Derick Berck	Windsor.
„ Richard Rich. *Drawing* .	Windsor.
„ Elizabeth Rich. *Drawing* . . .	Windsor.
„ the Same. *Half-length*	Buildwas.
„ Sir Edward Seymour	Sion House.
„ Sir John Russel. *Drawing* .	Windsor.
„ Same. *Oil Painting* . .	Woburn Abb
„ a Boy, Francis Russel. *Drawing* .	Windsor.
„ William Fitz-William. *Drawing*	Windsor.
„ Stanley, Earl of Derby. *Drawing* . .	Windsor.
„ Sir Thomas Strange. *Drawing* . .	Windsor.
„ Sir Thomas Wentworth. *Drawing* . .	Windsor.
„ Charles Wingfield. *Drawing* . . .	Windsor.
„ young Edward Clinton. *Drawing* . .	Windsor.
„ Thomas Parrie. *Drawing*	Windsor.
„ Philip Hobbie. *Drawiwg*	Windsor.
„ William Sherington. *Drawing* .	Windsor.
„ Sir Nicholas Carewe. *Oil Painting* .	Dalkeith Castle
„ Hubert Morett. *Oil Painting* . . .	Dresden Gall.
„ the Same. *Drawing*	Earl of Arundel
„ A Man (*probably by Holbein*) . . .	Petworth.
Henry VIII. at Table. *Drawing in Indian ink* . .	Brit. Mus.

1538.

Four Musicians. *Drawing*	Brit. Mus.
Woman with a Child on her Lap. *Drawing* . .	Brit. Mus.
Design for a Scabbard.	Bernburg.
„ for the Same	Basel.
„ for the Same. *Engraved by Loedel* . . .	Weigel Coll.
Designs for Dagger Sheaths	Brit. Mus.
„ for Ornament. *Mounted and framed* . .	Brit. Mus.
Sketch-book, with Designs. *Some marked* 1537 . .	Basel.
Sketch-book. *Known by Hollar's Engravings* . .	Lost.
Studies from Life	Basel.
Old Testament History. *Drawings from* . . .	Basel.
New Testament History. *Drawings from. Engraved* .	Basel.
Lady and Gentleman, kneeling	Basel.
Designs for Goldsmiths	Brit. Mus.
„ for Brooches, Earrings, Clasps, &c. . .	Brit. Mus.
„ for Sword-hilts	Basel.
„ for Sword-hilt. (*Engraved by W. Hollar*) .	
„ for Goblets, Drinking Vessels, &c. . .	Basel.
„ for Goblet for Hans of Antwerp . . .	Basel.
„ for Jane Seymour's Cup. *Large Drawing* .	Bodleian Lib.
„ the Same. *Sketch*	Brit. Mus.
Portrait of Prince Edward	Hanover.
„ the Same. *Drawing*	Windsor.
„ the Same. *Large painting* . . .	Sion House.
„ the Same. *Sketch intended for sculpture* .	Basel.
„ the Same. *Drawing*	Windsor.
„ of the Duchess of Milan	Arundel Castle
„ Anne of Cleves. *In crimson velvet dress* .	Louvre.
„ of the Same. *Miniature*	Goodrich Court

1540 AND 1541.

Portrait of Duke of Norfolk	Windsor.
„ Earl of Surrey. *Copied in Fruytiers's family picture of the Earl of Arundel* . .	Lord Stafford.
„ of the Same. *Drawing*	Windsor.
„ Catherine Howard. *Miniature* . . .	Windsor.
„ the Same. *Drawing*	Windsor.
„ a Young Man	Belvidere.
„ a Man, sixty years of age	Aix-la-Chapelle

1542.

Portrait of Sir William Parr	Windsor.
,, Lord Cobham	Windsor.
,, a Young Man. *Drawing*	Städel Mus.
,, a Youth	Hague.

1542 AND 1543.

King Henry VIII. granting a Charter to the Barber-Surgeons Guild. *Large painting*	Barber-Surgeons' Hall.
Portrait of Sir William Butts	Windsor.
,, Lady Butts	Mr. P. Carewe.
,, Sir John Chambers	Belvidere.
,, Himself. (*Engraved by W. Hollar*)	D. of Buccleuch
Portrait of Martin Luther. (*Bought in* 1879.)	Nat. Gallery.

CHRONOLOGY OF HANS HOLBEIN.

Date.		Page
1497.	Born at Ausburg	3
1515.	Residing in Basel	6
	Early Work	7
1517.	Living at Lucerne	14
	Returns to Basel	16
	Disturbances at Basel	42
1527.	Arrives in England	43
	Introduction to Sir Thomas More	48
1528.	Visits Basel	58
	His Wife and Children	60
1531.	Returns to England	63
1536.	Enters King Henry VIII.'s service	80
1538.	His Salary	90
1538-9.	Re-visits Basel, and returns to England	94
1543.	Dies in London of the Plague	102
	His Will	102

PICTURES BY HOLBEIN

SHEWN AT THE

EXHIBITION OF WORKS OF THE OLD MASTERS, 1880.

147.	Head of Old Man. *Fur round neck* . .	D. of Devonshire.
149.	Lady Vaux. *Holds a pink in her hand* . .	Hampton Court.
150.	Portrait of a Man. *Holds a pink in right hand*	D. of Devonshire.
152.	Henry Howard, Earl of Surrey . . .	Mr. Butler.
157.	Lady Heneage. *Black cap with white border* .	Mr. G. C. Handford.
161.	Henry VIII. *Left hand grasping a staff* .	D. of Devonshire.
162.	Portrait of a Child. *Blue and white dress* .	Sir H. A. Hoare.
163.	Edward VI. *As a child of two* . . .	D. of Northumberland.
167.	Lord Delaware. *Black dress slashed crimson* .	Mr. R. S. Holford.
168.	A German Lady	Earl Spencer.
169.	The Wheel of Fortune. *An allegorical picture*	D. of Devonshire.
170.	Portrait of a Man. *In crimson doublet* . .	Mr. J. E. Millais.
171.	Lady Guildford	Mr. Frewen.
172.	Derick Berck. "*An* 1536, *ÆT.* 30" . .	Lord Leconfield.
173.	Thomas Howard, Duke of Norfolk . .	D. of Norfolk.
174.	Sir Henry Guildford. *With collar of the garter*	Windsor.
175.	Sir William Butts. *Sable-lined cloak; gold chain*	Mr. W. H. Pole Carew.
177.	Christina of Denmark. *Full length* . .	D. of Norfolk.
178.	Lady Butts. *Diamond shape head-dress* . .	Mr. W. H. Pole Carew.
179.	William of Warham, Archbishop of Canterbury	Lambeth Palace.
180.	Thomas Howard, 3rd Duke of Norfolk . .	Windsor.
181.	John, Elector of Saxony. *Steel chain around neck*	Mr. R. S. Holford.
182.	Sir John More. *Holds a letter in left hand* .	E. of Pembroke.
183.	A Merchant of the Steelyard	Windsor.
184.	A Young Man. *Left hand holding a glove* .	Mr. George P. Boyce.
185.	John Reskimer. *Long red beard* . . .	Hampton Court.
187.	"Noli me tangere"	Hampton Court.
188.	Sir Brian Tuke. *Gold chain and cross round neck*	M. of Westminster.
190.	Anton Fugger. *Holds a book in right hand* .	Mr. Francis Cook.
191.	John Herbster. *Painter of Basle* . . .	E. of Northbrook.
192.	Sir Nicholas Carew. *In armour* . . .	D. of Buccleuch.
195.	Princess Elizabeth. *Holds a book in her hands*	St. James's Palace.
198.	A Young Man. *With black cap and cloak* .	D. of Marlborough.
203.	William Tell. *An imaginary portrait* . .	Sir Philip Miles.
204.	Thomas Cromwell, Earl of Essex. "*ÆT.* 14, *AN°. DN.* 1515"	D. of Devonshire.
205.	Thomas Howard, Duke of Norfolk . . .	D. of Devonshire.
237.	Edward VI. on Horseback. *In armour* . .	D. of Buccleuch.

* In the *Athenæum* of January, 1880, there are important notices of this exhibition. Several of these pictures are of doubtful authenticity.

INDEX.

(*The names of Paintings and Woodcuts are in Italics.*)

Page

Adam and Eve 12
Adoration of the Magi, The . . 31
Alphabet of Children (*Woodcuts*) 24
Alphabet of Death (*Woodcuts*) . 24
Ambassadors, The 72
Amerbach, Bonifacius, Portrait 16
Anne of Cleves 96
Augsburg, City of 2

Basel, Town of . . . 6, 15, 17, 43
Basel, Famine at 63
Bebel, Palma 26
Bible Illustrations (*Woodcuts*) . 76
Book Illustrations (*Woodcuts*) . 25
Burgkmaer, Hans 2

Carew, Sir Nicholas, Portrait of 85
Carlsruhe, Kunsthalle . . . 32
Chambers, Dr. John, Portrait of 101
Charter of the Barber-Surgeons' Company 100
Chesemon, Robert, Portrait of . 73
Cleves, The Duchess of . . . 96
Cratander, Andreas 26
Cromwell, Thomas, Portraits of 74
Curio, Valentin 26

Dance of Death, The (*Woodcuts*) 19
Dead Christ, The 30
Designs for Ornament by Holbein 88
Duchess of Milan, Portrait of . 89

Edward, Prince, Portraits of . 95
Erasmus' Visit to Basel . . . 8
Erasmus, Portraits of . . 38, 39, 62

Fisher, Bishop of Rochester . . 51
Fountain of Health, The . . 15
Freiburg Cathedral, Altar-piece 31
Froben, Johann . . . 8, 24, 26
Froschover, Christoph . . . 26

Godsalve, Sir Thomas, and his Son 52
Guildford, Sir Henry and Lady 51
Gyze, Jörg, Portrait of . . . 64

Henry VIII. and his Father . . 81
Henry VIII. at Table . . . 86
Henry VIII., Miniatures of . 82
Herbster, Hans, Portrait of . . 12
Hertenstein, Herr 14
Hobbie, Philip 89
Holbein, Ambrosius . . 3, 12

Page

Holbein, Hans, the elder . . 3
Holbein, Michael 3
Holbein, Sigismund 3
Holbein's Wife and Children . 60
Holbein, Portraits of . . 40, 101
Holy Birth, The 31
Horebout, Lucas . . 47

Jane Seymour, Queen, Portrait. 82
Jane Seymour Cup, The . . . 87
John of Antwerp, Portrait of . 66

Kratzer, Nicolas, Portrait of . 52

Lucerne, Wall-paintings at . . 14
Luther, Martin, Portrait of . . 99
Lützelberger, Hans 19

Man of Sorrows, The 30
Melancthon, Portrait of . . . 38
Merchants of the Steelyard . . 67
Meyer of Hasen and his Wife . 10
Meyer Madonna, The . . . 33, 35
More, Sir Thomas 42
More, Sir Thomas, Portraits of. 49
More, Family of Sir Thomas . 54
Morett, Hubert, Portrait of . . 86
Mother of Sorrows, The . . . 30

Norfolk, The Duke of, Portrait of 97

Oberriedt, Councillor 31
Old Testament Pictures (*Woodcuts*) 61

Passion, The, Drawings of . . 12
Peasants' Alphabet (*Woodcuts*) . 24

Page

Peasants' Dance, The (*Woodcut*) 17
Petri, Adam 26
Portraits Un-named . 15, 52, 53, 72, 74, 83, 99
Praise of Folly, Illustrations of 8

Rich, Elizabeth, Portrait of . . 84
Ruskin, John 64

St. George 32
St. Sebastian, Altar-piece of . 3
St. Ursula 32
Satirical Woodcuts . . 77
Scholars, The 73
Schongauer, Martin . . . 2
Schweiger, Jörg, Portrait of 13
Seymour, Sir Edward, Portrait 84
Solothurn Madonna, The . 33
Southwell, Sir Richard . . . 84

Title-Pages (*Woodcuts*) . . 25, 26
Triumphs of Riches and Poverty 69
Tuke, Sir Bryan, Portraits of . 53

Vaux, Lady, Portrait of . . 83

Warham, Archbishop 50
Weigel Collection 34
Wheel of Fortune, The . . . 68
Windsor Drawings, The . . 47, 67, 71, 75, 88
Windsor Drawings, Autotypes 48
Wood Engravings 27
Wyat, Sir Thomas . . . 50, 73

Zurich Table, The 7

www.ingramcontent.com/pod-product-compliance
Lightning Source LLC
Chambersburg PA
CBHW021123020726
47500CB00003B/903
* 9 7 8 3 3 3 7 3 9 4 8 6 8 *